Penguin Books
The Last Best Friend

George Sims was born in London in 1923, and was
educated at the Lower School of John Lyon, Harrow. He
served for five years in a Special Communications Unit in
the Army, and then became a dealer in rare books and
manuscripts. He enjoys travelling, particularly in the
Mediterranean and the West Indies, where he can practise
his hobby of underwater swimming. He likes driving fast
cars and is also interested in the cinema. His previous
novels, *The Terrible Door* (1964) and *Sleep No More* (1966),
are available in Penguins, and his fourth novel, *The Sand
Dollar*, was published in 1969. George Sims and his wife
Beryl have three children. They live in Berkshire.

George Sims

The Last Best Friend

Penguin Books

Penguin Books Ltd, Harmondsworth,
Middlesex, England
Penguin Books Australia Ltd, Ringwood,
Victoria, Australia

First published by Victor Gollancz 1967
Published in Penguin Books 1971
Copyright © George Sims, 1967

Made and printed in Great Britain by
Hazell Watson & Viney Ltd
Aylesbury, Bucks
Set in Linotype Baskerville

To Réne & Doris Quero

'My name is Death; the last best Friend am I'
Robert Southey

'Somehow in the case of Jews I always suspect suicide'
James Joyce

I

2 p.m., Monday, 1st August, 1966. Paddington, London.

Vertigo? 'Giddiness, dizziness (in which the patient feels as if he, as if surrounding objects, were turning round).' The small man standing on the the narrow ledge stared fixedly forward with eyes made wide and blank by terror. His face was ashen and veins stood out in his forehead as though he was straining to vomit. Very slowly he edged one foot sideways without looking down, but the move-ment was indecisive and feeble like that of a dying insect and he brought it back clumsily so that for a second he trod the terrifying emptiness that lay before him. When both feet were together again there was a sudden move-ment in his dark brown eyes, spiralling down to meet the treacherous, shifting surfaces of roofs and streets which be-gan to spin below him. As they gathered speed his left arm was pressed ever tighter against the wall's smooth stone blocks and his fingers scrabbled uselessly at the hardly perceptible divisions while he pushed at the air with an upraised right hand in an equally futile effort to steady himself.

Suicide? 'Person who intentionally kills himself.' The small man winced, shutting his eyes and cringing as though he had been punched in the stomach. His face was already streaked with greasy marks and sweat ran down steadily through his thin black hair to join drops which beaded his long top lip. He held his eyes tightly closed while he wrenched frantically at his tie, pulling it loose and tearing off the collar button, breathing noisily through his mouth with a gasping sound. Slowly his body began to sway backwards and forwards like a pendulum, taking up an apparently irresistible rhythm, a momentum to join with that of the crazy switchback ride over dizzy heights and depths which was taking place inside his brain. When he opened his eyes they showed despair but also some kind of resolution – his mouth was set firm, he lifted his chin and made a tiny gesture of defiance. He shouted something incoherently, leant forward at an angle impossible for recovery, appearing to defy the force of gravity for a second or so, then fell, uttering a single short cry, a noise which did not sound particularly human, simply the ignominious yelp of an animal encountering death.

2 p.m., Monday, 1st August, 1966. Calvi, Corsica.

'Ned, are you asleep?'

Balfour woke with a sensation of some grievous but hardly definable loss, just a dim sense of vanished beauty, and then, momentarily, a brief fragment of his dream returned – it had been a delightful little nod off, a glimpse of an Arcadian world where personality did not persist.

'You were asleep. You absolute no-goodnik. Quelle insult!'

'Definitely *not* an insult,' Balfour said rather indistinctly, still nuzzling the girl's shoulder which had the hue and texture of an apricot rose. 'The opposite in fact. I was charmed and lulled.'

Already the dream's atmosphere of complete tranquillity, such as he never experienced in his waking life, was vanishing irrecoverably, leaving only the vague and inadequate impression of a river's surface glinting like gold in autumn sunlight. Another kind of vanishing trick had taken place as well. Where were the impatient lovers who had entered this darkened room, oblivious of their surroundings, leaving a meal half-finished, intoxicated with something stronger than wine, exchanging ever deeper kisses of an intense fig-like sweetness? What had become of that mutual madness which dictated such frantic undressing, deep sighs, lascivious embraces? The passionate lovers had disappeared, and in their place there was an indolent amiable girl and a middle-aged man with 'a selfish expression' and a scarred body. The tall, brass-framed mirror on the facing wall would have recorded, momentarily, all their hectic goings-on: if it had been a camera instead how ludicrous, even faintly sinister, a film of those few minutes would now appear – truly a study of *folie à deux*.

Balfour looked round the room: he had pushed Bunty through the first door that came to hand when they had emerged from the kitchen, entwined and slowly moving together like a clumsy animal; it was the one formerly used by the du Cros' ancient aunt, now dead; it still contained a number of her possessions, mostly valueless bric-à-brac of the highly personal kind which is an embarrassment to relatives. In the room darkened by plastic mosquito shutters her pathetic treasures had taken on a depressing and slightly macabre aspect. There was another, smaller mirror in a passepartout frame, and they were also regarded by the daguerreotype of a grim-faced bearded *poilu*. On a sun-bleached rosewood table there was a disordered array of sea-shells, dusty invitations in outmoded typefaces, a chipped bonbonnière decorated with cherubs, and a Japanese fan. Balfour felt a long-dormant memory stirring in him, something at first inexpressible – then he recalled the odd and distinct smell of a similar oiled paper fan which he had found many years before in a box belonging to his mother.

'Round and round the garden, went the teddy bear . . .' Bunty tickled Balfour's hand, breaking his reverie. She looked and smelt delicious – again like a rose, the André Le Troquer – but Balfour knew that further love-making would necessitate some acting on his part as he felt remote and slightly unreal; at first he blamed this on the rather claustrophobic atmosphere of the room, with its pointless collection of mementoes testifying to the fleetingness and futility of life; then, with a momentary flash of self-candour, he realized that this was just a subterfuge, an attempt to excuse a middle-aged man's failing ardour.

He raised himself on his left arm and pushed her back firmly with his right hand, extending his fingers in a gently clawing motion like a cat. His heavily muscled arm held her prisoner, lying across her belly with his fingers pointing at the teardrop pearl which hung from a thin gold chain. The small erect nipples stood out like raspberry grains. It would make a good painting – the contrast between the thin brown hand, vigorous and masculine, and the cream-coloured breasts, the quintessential image of womanhood, of passivity and defencelessness. Already the hand showed some signs of ageing – there were tiny silver hairs in among the sun-bleached ones, and a few 'grave' marks. In twenty or thirty years it would be an old man's hand, then after a few more years it would be burnt in an oven – a prospect he viewed with reasonable equanimity. Meanwhile it reached out for a share of the good things. 'Let each man take up his chisel and inscribe his fate ...'

Bunty lifted herself up on her elbows and regarded him dispassionately. 'First of all you fall asleep on me, now you seem about a million miles away. I like not ye man who ...'

'Well, what can you expect if you will take up with an aged gent?' Balfour countered. He traced the faint impressions of her ribs, sensuously enjoying the fullness and weight of her breasts pressing against the back of his hand. 'What I like is this pearl between two rubies ...' He broke off abruptly, lifting his head like a cat sensing danger and holding up a hand in a silencing gesture. 'I think I hear somebody.'

Bunty sprang from the bed, picking up Balfour's butcher-blue shirt: with this held in front of her she advanced cautiously to the french windows which opened on to a low balcony and partly dislodged the green plastic mosquito screen.

'Lord! It's my Mama. Quelle fate.'

Her tone of alarm petered out so that finally she did not sound too worried. 'So what do we do now? Hide under the bed? I presume you've had lots of experience.'

'Nasty.' Balfour took back his shirt and gave her a light smack. 'Well, we can't keep her waiting there. The heat is terrific. I'll go out ...'

Bunty grinned. 'Public prejudice runs to at least one more garment.'

Balfour grimaced and pulled on his dark blue swimming trunks, keeping Mrs Hillyard in view as she walked along the path, closely surveying the villa.

When he stepped on to the balcony the brilliance of the light-diffused scene forced him to hold a hand above his eyes. There was no sign of the brief rainstorm that had taken place before lunch and the atmosphere was again oppressive; the sky was a flat blue like a child's painting and light shimmered on the sea and the distant Citadel and the cluster of white, beige and pink-washed buildings that was Calvi. The green tiles were so hot that it was painful to walk on them with bare feet and he moved gingerly on arched soles to the shallow steps which led down to the garden.

Mrs Hillyard stood on the stony path that was patterned with tough, feather-headed weeds. She wore a sleeveless canary-coloured cotton dress; her arms were badly sunburnt and her shoulders were covered with a white chiffon scarf. Fanning her face with a sprig of rosemary, with occasional swipes at some persistent insect, she looked very hot and uncomfortable. There were no trees in the parched-looking garden to give shade and the air was filled with the continuous noise of cicadas and loudly buzzing flies. She whistled faintly.

'I knew it would be hot in Corsica but this is like being trapped in an oven.' She gestured vaguely. 'Is this yours?' Her tone was intended to be light but it was tinged with envy and something else which Balfour could not pinpoint.

'No – alas. It belongs to some friends of mine who live in Paris, Roger and Françoise du Cros. I expect you'll meet them in a week or so.' He noticed that there were mosquito bites on her arms and her hands were red and swollen.

'I wondered – if you'd seen Bunty.' This time her voice was sharply suspicious. Balfour met her look directly and replied quickly and honestly – evasions that avoided lying usually came easily to him:

'I saw her swimming at the Sun Beach this morning. And she said something about water-skiing this afternoon.'

'Water-skiing!' Mrs Hillyard's eyes blazed with irritation. 'Really, that girl! She went off this morning without a word so naturally we thought she would be back for lunch. She knew we had hired a car and planned to go to Piana this afternoon.'

'Do come in for a moment and have a cool drink.' Balfour touched the back of her hand lightly, then pointed at the elegant white villa, with doors and shutters painted heliotrope, where she was staying. The garden there was shaded by giant palm-trees; it was regularly watered and tended throughout the year, unlike the du Cros' which was not touched from October to Easter. 'You've been weeding that magnificent garden.' There was a hint of an accusation in the way he said this.

'You're right, though I don't know how you guessed. It's so pleasantly cool there in the evening before the mosquitos descend and I can't resist pottering.'

Balfour pointed at the tiny bumps on her fingers: 'Those are not mosquito bites – they're minute insects – I don't know what the French name is, but in Dorset they call them harvesters. Painful and very irritating I know by experience. Bathe your hands here while I get you some iced *ananas*.'

Mrs Hillyard went up the steps and through the front door, pausing for a moment and looking into the large room on her right with its series of french windows and views of the Golfe de Calvi and the Citadel. He put his hand on her back and she turned to him, cautiously smiling:

'That's rather super. Must be wonderful at night.'

She hesitated again at the end of the passage where there was a closed door on her right leading to the kitchen and patio, and a passage to the left with the doors of the five bedrooms. For a moment Balfour did not guide her. He was experiencing a light-headed feeling that often came to him in tricky situations: an indifference that was tantamount to a wish for danger, exposure and failure. Sammy Weiss called it 'the will for self-destruction'. He felt that he did not really care if she turned left, forcing him to take part in a kind of French farce. But there was something else which had caused him to pause. When he had put his hand on her back she had shivered and as their eyes met there had been a momentary expression of attraction – a message so fleeting that afterwards one wondered if it had appeared. He did find her attractive – she had the same widely spaced dark blue eyes, clusters of freckles and firm jaw as Bunty. She smelt rather deliciously of Pears soap and dianthus talc. For a moment he had been tempted to slip his arm round her waist, and then was disturbed by this impulse. Barbara had said: 'You're sick. It's an illness. There's a name for it.' It was true that he had always found many women attractive; he was not the type to make a faithful husband. But this casual, practically automatic, lust provoked by a smile and a moment's intimacy was a new development, and one he did not like. Was Barbara's diagnosis true – would he become a tiresome old Don Juan, always touching women, making advances to see if they would be repulsed?

He opened the kitchen door and turned on the tap with an abstracted air. Mrs Hillyard's gaze became suspicious again, directed at the table in the dining alcove set for two, the plates untidy with scraps of ham and olives, a bowl containing the remains of a *gazpacho* salad, glasses half-filled with rosé wine.

'Marie-Antoinette, the maid,' he explained, rather too quickly. 'She wanted to go down to the Lido so I said I would wash up, after my siesta. She's not too hot at washing-up, but a splendid cook, comes from Brittany, does a marvellous *gigot de pré-salé*. You must all come for dinner some time.'

'That's very kind,' she said non-committally. Her renewed suspicion had completely dispersed the air of intimacy; her eyes were watchfully attentive and Balfour wondered if Bunty had left anything identifiable by the table – he had begun to undress her there but only, as far as he could remember, to the extent of undoing the shoulder buttons on her terry towelling beach frock.

'You've stayed here before?'

'Yes, twice – but with my family then.'

'Oh – you're married.' Again her tone was intended to be light and unconcerned but it was obvious that she had given the matter some thought and was surprised that he should be willing to confirm her suspicions, as if he had casually given her a weapon which could be used against him.

'Yes – but we're separated.' His automatic, not very friendly grin and quizzical expression demanded how long this questioning would continue. She put down the glass of *ananas*.

'Many thanks. It seems we shall have to make the trip to Piana daughterless. If by any chance you should happen to see her, perhaps you'll say we shan't be back till seven or so.'

He stood at the top of the steps blinking in the brilliant sunlight, then shading his eyes frowningly to make a pause for thought; but a phrase to pass over the tricky situation eluded him and after a moment she walked off, with a brief wave of her hand. He watched her until she had gone over the first little bridge and past the clump of eucalyptus trees, then he turned back and went down the dark and comparatively cool passage.

Bunty had removed one of the screens and put on her polka-dot bikini; she was sitting in a cane chair, reading an old copy of *Paris-Match*. She regarded him over the top of steel-rimmed dark glasses which were perched half-way down her nose. The look was at once provocative and critical. What was she thinking? That he was practically her mother's contemporary? That someone her own age would be more fun? He could dive, swim and water-ski better than most of the youngsters on the beach, his sense of humour was still functioning off and on, and no one had ever accused him of taking life too seriously, but he was well aware of his limitations as far as she was concerned. Above all he lacked her true, spontaneous gaiety – and there were occasions when she seemed like an inhabitant of a different planet, instead of a member of another generation, and it was as if he could not possibly communicate with her. Perhaps her appraising look meant that he was for the chop. If so he could not grumble. That was the way they had agreed to play the game.

He patted the bed. 'Come here.'

Bunty cleared her throat and raised her eyebrows in a meaningful way and said 'I've been there,' but she put down the magazine and approached him rather coyly. He pulled her on to his knees, humming a brief snatch of *Baubles, Bangles and Beads*, then made a fuss of fingering the pearl, raising his eyebrows like Groucho Marx and saying: 'Yes, Madam, an eighteen grain orient drop on a fine trace. Worth ...'

'Yes. Worth how much?'

'Who gave it to you?'

'My old man. For my twenty-first. Can you really value it?'

'I could hazard a fairly intelligent guess. I've a friend who is a jeweller and he's told me a lot. But this seems to be the occasion for one of my rare moments of tact. Let us say you could not buy it for £200 – a fine pearl. And not a bad bit of skin come to that ...'

Bunty was cradled in his left arm. Her eyebrows looked as if they had just been dashed on in pale gold; the fine strokes glistened against her deeply tanned forehead. He tugged gently at the lobes of her ears and pretended to have difficulty in getting her face in the right position for a kiss. He was just bending down to complete this enjoyably protracted business when she gave a start: 'What the hell's that?'

She pointed dramatically to the ceiling. He looked up to see what appeared to be the elongated shadow of a man's torso. For a moment it was stationary, then it jerked forward and down out of their vision. Some chance arrangement of mirrors and lenses had contrived a *camera obscura* effect to present them with this startling image. Once gone it seemed impossible that it had in fact been there, but Bunty was not in any doubt. She squirmed out of his arms and on to her knees on the floor. 'Christ! First my Mama. Now we have a voyeur out there!'

Balfour moved quickly to the open window, to see a postman straightening up from tying his shoe-lace. The man was sweating profusely and kept dabbing his forehead with a grubby handkerchief. He was obviously annoyed at having had to make this trip which necessitated a steep walk up from the rough track. He muttered something about a telegram and an inadequate address, and then frowned as if searching for something else to say to unburden more of his irritation. He pushed an envelope at Balfour with an aggressive movement which displayed a large black area round the armpit of his faded uniform.

Cables were a daily occurrence in Balfour's business but he was faintly disturbed at receiving one on holiday: he had left instructions that he was not to be sent any communications from his office – it flashed through his mind that this might be something about one of the children, an accident perhaps.

The telegram was addressed simply to Balfour, care of du Cros, Calvi, Corsica. It read: VITAL I HAVE YOUR ADVICE ON TERRIBLE DECISION I MUST MAKE PLEASE PHONE ME TOMORROW MORNING AT THE ARCADE AS EVER SAMMY WEISS. Balfour was not aware of the postman leaving as he stood re-reading the form, slowly digesting its scanty, puzzling message.

3

While Bunty tidied the bedroom and put the dishes in the sink, Balfour drove the battered grey Citroen 'two-horse' round to the front of the villa, arranged two pairs of water-skis in the back and fetched an air-mattress for the girl to sit on as only the driver's seat remained in the car. He went through these actions automatically, his mind preoccupied with the message from Sammy Weiss which was so curiously out of character as to seem spurious; in the fourteen years they had known each other there had been innumerable occasions when he had asked Sammy's advice, but he could not remember a single occasion when the positions had been reversed; the situation was made even odder and more ironic by the fact that it was due to Sammy offering him some, for once, unwanted advice that they had not met during the week before he went on holiday. Looking for bathing towels he realized that his mind was going round and round pointlessly as it sometimes did in the early hours of the morning, laboriously from point A to B to C and then with a jump back exactly to A. This was due to a feeling of frustration: he liked tackling problems of any kind, but if they came up he wanted to start on them immediately and this time it was not possible – for some unknown reason Sammy had insisted on him phoning the next day, which meant he would have about eighteen hours of indecision and useless speculation.

Driving down the steep slope and then along the narrow track was like negotiating an obstacle course. There were many large holes to skirt, and two places where rough bridges had been made from concrete slabs to cross the culvert which brought the water from the mountains, and these had to be treated with respect even if one was not concerned about the car.

Usually he enjoyed the bumpy drive with *maquis*-scented air coming in through the open roof, chestnut tree branches dipping almost to the top of the car and eucalyptus trees humming with bees. Even the oppressive heat in the car was made bearable by knowing that the journey led to the sea, but with the enigmatic telegram still nagging at his mind (surely it could only mean that S. was in some very serious though unimaginable danger/difficulty? Possibly a serious illness but why should he then want to consult him?) it now seemed rather flat and pointless.

'Is it true – that you drove – this, this vehicle – down the steps – at Île Rousse?' Bunty asked, grimly holding the side of the car but still bumping up and down, and occasionally rising out of contact with the lilo as the old 'deux chevaux' rattled along like a tank. Balfour nodded and grinned: 'The story that I drove it back up again from the Café des Platanes is exaggerated.' He could sense more than see that she was regarding him appraisingly again; she leant over and touched some of the small scars which circled his throat like a necklace and made smooth hairless places on his chest – the skin there was thin and wrinkled, like a dead leaf.

'Did this hurt terribly? Being burnt like that – it's something one can't imagine.'

'Yes and no. Not just when it happened, and then I had some morphine shots and blacked out – but boy it caught up with me later on.'

She traced the large scar below his ribs: 'This is like Ireland. An archipelago round your neck. South America on your thigh. Squashed Australia or somewhere on your foot. Why is it all on one side?'

'It was in the war – in Italy. A lorry full of jerrycans of petrol exploded. I was a wireless operator and we worked from a mobile transmitter called a "gin palace" – I'd gone off to make some tea when the convoy stopped. Some shells came down and our lorry was hit, and then I hope I was running back when the petrol went up whoosh!'

'Hope?' Bunty exclaimed.

'Yes, hope. I don't really know what I was doing. I might well have been streaking off – but I had two friends in that lorry and I hope I was trying to help them. Completely futile anyway as they were both dead but if I was trying that was my sole contribution to the war – we were only in Italy for five weeks, just four days within the sound of the German guns. The rest of the war I was swanning round England . . .'

He was on the verge of telling her of his abiding feeling of guilt and regret for not having done more in the war, but he rejected it just in time as putting too much weight on their flimsy relationship; it was required of him to amuse her as far as he was able, not regurgitate all this old stuff. The day before he had nearly asked her to remove some sea-urchin spines from his foot, as Barbara had often done on other Mediterranean holidays, but he had had a sudden vision of himself holding up a yellowing, hard-skinned sole for her to poke at with a needle, visualized a delicate cat's yawn in response, and swallowed the request.

Turning past the veronica hedge on to the sand-covered road, Balfour determined to stop talking about himself and stop thinking about the cable – it was fruitless to brood on what it might mean and it could not help Sammy. They had an afternoon and evening to enjoy – water-skiing, swimming and then dinner, perhaps at 'Le Coucou' *pizzeria*. He drove quite fast over the yielding surface of the parking area, swerving round the *mobile crêperie* so that he had sufficient momentum to run up the slope and park right under the umbrella pines. It was good to feel the dry sand and pine-needles under his feet as he unloaded the skis, pleasant to have the sun beating on his back and know that the sea was only fifty feet away. 'Who doth ambition shun, And loves to live i' the sun.'

As they walked past the queue of children waiting for

pancakes Balfour noticed two youths standing at the gap in the pines which led to the beach, and then saw one turn as if to signal to someone behind him. When they went over the single railway-track half buried in sand they saw they had quite a large audience of teenagers, sitting close together as if waiting for a show.

'I say, this isn't fair,' Bunty complained. 'I shall never get up with that bunch there. I do it badly enough without any critical eyes watching me.'

'Nonsense,' Balfour replied firmly. 'You'll show them. Just relax. Don't forget to concentrate on keeping the skis straight as you start, then bring them closer together as they begin to plane.'

It was absurd, but he very much wanted her to get up on the skis at the first attempt with this group watching. There was something about a clique of wealthy French youngsters with their snobbishness, determined modishness and arrogance which irritated him, bringing out chauvinistic feelings. He decided to give them something to watch, and walked on his hands down to the firm sand at the sea's edge despite a disapproving exclamation from Bunty. There was some derisive slow hand-clapping and a few jeering comments: *'Amusez-vous bien!' 'C'est bien fait pour vous!' 'Le temps est arrivé!'*

As he flipped on to his feet he wanted to make a small bow to his apparently hostile audience but this effect was destroyed as his right foot, already made sore by the removal of sea-urchin spines, connected with a sharp stone. The pain was quite intense for a moment and he hopped twice, then dissembled his discomfiture by plunging into the shallow water.

When he got up again the young man who owned the boat was wading in with the ski lines. The Boston Whaler was the powerful *'modèle sport'* which could easily pull two skiers. There was a smallish figure with a white yachting-cap seated hunched behind the wheel staring fixedly out to sea and another youth in a bathing-costume bending over the ropes at the stern.

Balfour pointed to the boat: *'Il est prêt, le bateau?'*

'Oui, monsieur.'

'Tu ne conduit pas, alors?'

'Non, monsieur, pas cet après-midi.'

The owner of the boat turned away, grimacing as if these questions were irritating and absurd. Balfour was puzzled why this man who the day before had been so helpful about Bunty's progress with water-skiing should now be surly and anxious for someone else to take over the boat. He said, *'Bon. Merci,'* and went to fetch the water-skis. He called out to Bunty: 'Remember, rope between the skis, tips just out of the water and about ten inches apart. Knees up to your chest. Wrists well spaced on the bar with knuckles uppermost.' As he gave this advice there were more unfriendly and derisive shouts from the beach: *'On se verra plus tard'*, *'A bientôt,'* *'Monsieur, monsieur, bon voyage!'*, and when the Boston whaler moved off there was an ironic roar from their audience.

Bunty was pulling on the rope a little too hard so that her feet shot forward and she nearly went over backwards. Balfour shouted, 'Keep your arms rigid. Don't tighten up.' He could see her nod and knew it was going to be all right. Then he looked in front again and noticed that the youth in the white cap had turned and was grinning, pointing first at the skiers and then meaningfully at the horizon; with a dull kind of shock he realized it was one of the boys with whom he had scuffled the previous evening at the café 'Chez Tao'. Balfour motioned his head at Bunty but the youth only shrugged and gunned the engine.

Balfour sniffed – he had a tight feeling in his nose and chest, warning signals that came to him before the red mist of anger. He shouted, 'Turn back or I'll give you another clip. *Arrête-toi! Tu veux que je te casse la gueule?'* The boy in the black trunks roared with laughter.

Balfour knew that his words could not be heard but

this did not stop him from shouting; his abuse became stronger after a quick glance at Bunty showed she realized this was not going to be an ordinary trip. Balfour was a good skier and could take a long and bumpy trip, but Bunty had only just started to learn; her face was taut and pale. They were going at such a clip he did not like to tell her to let go. He bunched a fist and shook it: 'Idiot. Saleté. Con! Espèce de con!' The boy in the costume just jigged about in response, waving and making funny faces. Balfour could not remember him but from his animosity it seemed that he too must have been involved in the fracas 'Chez Tao'. He took deep breaths and inwardly cursed himself. Did anyone else of his age get involved in affairs like this leading to a teenage vendetta?

At first it seemed as if they might be going straight out but then the boat swung left from the *Golfe de Revellata*, round the point and sped due south past the *Grotte les Veaux Marins*, running parallel with the corniche to Porto and Piana. The boy leaning over the back of the boat had been watching Bunty while he was fooling about and now he called out to the other youth, pointing in to one of the little bays which dotted the coast. The boat made a tight turn, swinging the skiers out in a wide arc. When they were in easy swimming distance of the rocks Balfour shouted, '*Let go*, Bunty, just let go,' raising one hand to show his intention. After the tension of the previous ten minutes, to drop the rope and ski in, slowly sinking as he lost momentum, was like falling back into an armchair.

They dogpaddled slowly in to the shore, laboriously pushing their skis in front of them, then lay side by side on a smooth white rock which looked in profile like a man's head with a prognathous jaw and a low forehead; their backs were arched over this simian brow and their rib cases pumped up and down like twin engines on a bench.

The motor-boat turned once more and the boys waved and shouted – their words did not carry but the jubilance did. Last night Balfour had intruded into their special, enclosed world because he had thought they were frightening a girl and in the ensuing fight he had hurt them – now they had marooned him perhaps three miles from Calvi on a rock ledge with a seemingly impenetrable barrier of bushes and briars which stretched right to the cliff top.

Bunty spoke for the first time since the hectic ride began: 'We're here because we're here because we're here.' Her voice was slightly shaky but she began to laugh. 'Your face when you realized. Such frustration. I thought you might go off pop!' She laughed again and Balfour joined in even though it hurt his ribs to do so. There was indeed something farcical about their situation and certainly the image of himself trying to be intimidating while being dragged along balanced on two small pieces of wood was ludicrous. Their laughter became unrestrained and went on until it became really painful.

When Balfour got up he felt quite weak. The boat was out of sight and the cove so silent that his voice sounded self-conscious and slightly theatrical.

'God, what a nut I was to interfere like that last night. That girl I "rescued" was there this afternoon you know. And the little bitch was laughing as we shot off. What a great idiot I am ...'

'Well you see she was probably enjoying being pulled about. I mean, in sight of the club there was no real danger. All the thrill of being ravished without any of the pain. Just screams of pleasurable excitement I suppose. Still, at the time I thought you were right to stop them. They were quite drunk and it *could* have become nasty.'

Balfour was mentally kicking himself all the way back to Calvi. It was nice of Bunty to try and defend his behaviour but he had handled the affair all wrong: Max Weber could have dealt with it in a commanding fashion, Sammy Weiss with a joking word, but he had acted at the youths' own level, pushing in and then punching hard as soon as they hit out at him. It seemed as if he would never grow up.

When he got up from the rock and looked down at the girl who was staring pensively up at the sky, he realized with a little jolt of surprise how similar her mouth was to Barbara's – the top lip was exactly the same, sharply outlined and not full but with a hint of sensitivity – the slight tremulousness which he had often seen much magnified on the cinema screen in close-ups of Julie Harris. And similar eyes, too, large and Aegean blue. He thought that perhaps he was always searching for the romantic, unworldly personality which should be mirrored by such eyes and that kind of mouth, but then some detached judicial part of his brain intervened to object – absurd self-delusion! Yet there was something about her expression which appealed deeply to him.

The sea was so clear and still momentarily that he could survey it far out like a giant aquarium until a breeze broke the glass-like surface into innumerable fragments. A ledge of rock extended from the point where he stood and there the water was only five or six feet deep, dropping at its edge to perhaps twenty. He searched the gently waving banks of light green weed and tempting channels of clear water above white sand; in the penumbra of the rock ledge he saw some *corbes* and *dorades* hugging clumps of darker weed. He had become absorbed in his search and oblivious of his surroundings. He turned to explain to Bunty: 'I must have a dip to cool off. Untie these knots of frustration.'

She nodded and he took a deep breath before plunging in. He kept his dive shallow over the ledge and then swam down strongly with a sensation of complete freedom, usually only found in dreams. The lure of the sea, indeed of any water, for Balfour was an atavistic thing, a yearning for the immeasurable and unknowable. Also there was the illusion he had in its depths of making a fresh start, of becoming someone with a purpose in life instead of being merely trapped in the flimsy webs of vanity and sexuality.

He held himself stationary by grasping strands of dark

red seaweed in both hands and then somersaulted so that his feet, looking enormous, stood momentarily on the white sand of the sea-floor and slimy yellow weed clung to his legs like a perverted embrace. With lungs bursting he jumped and propelled himself with kicking legs to the surface. As he broke through to the sunlight and took in air he experienced a marvellous sense of well-being, a feeling of having shed the heavy though unformulated sense of guilt he toted round like a pack. This would not last – it would be brief, he knew himself well enough for that, but for the time being it was like drinking several glasses of champagne.

He pushed the skis as far as possible under a bush and arranged them so that the ends were hidden by a clump of mesembryanthemum. He pointed to the cliff top: 'We'll soon be up there. I've been to lots of these coves with Roger du Cros and there is always a criss-cross path. Yes, you see! It starts there. What do you think?'

Bunty grinned weakly: 'Quite smashing.' It was a phrase they had taken over secretly from a Junoesque German girl who held court at the *Café du Golfe*, using her own brand of British slang. She shook her head nervously from side to side as the Berliner did and mimicked again: 'Some bit of a drag.'

After only a few steps Balfour was sweating and dirty. The refreshing effect of his swim was soon lost as he struggled to climb the badly overgrown path. The *maquis* which covered the cliffs seemed to be mainly composed of briars and thorn bushes, and the recent rainstorm had left it slippery underfoot without dispersing a black dust which clung to the intractable branches. Cluster-flies, brown bees and other insects hovered along the path, descending on his head when he needed both hands to break off giant thistles or push a briar into a position from which it would not spring out at Bunty. There was one point where he had to climb a section as the path had fallen away, and he could do this only by gripping whin-bushes. He remembered ascending similar paths with Roger du Cros after under-water swimming expeditions and thinking nothing of them, but with feet, arms and chest bare this ascent was as unpleasant as the youths had intended it should be.

When they reached the top they slumped down by the side of the road. Balfour put a grubby, badly scratched hand round Bunty's shoulders. 'Thanks for not grumbling. You're a good sport.' Then he laughed: 'Terribly clipped and British that praise. But seeing you've had to go all through this and you were only a bystander last night, I really mean it.' It struck him that the caress had been one that a father or uncle might make.

'Sounds like high praise in fact. And when I've got cleaned up I shan't mind. . . . It was rather an adventure. Once I've had a shower. . . . But I hope there won't be any more chapters. So no retaliation now!'

Balfour shook his head firmly. 'No – I was tempted – particularly when one briar went right inside my nose. But I was in the wrong the other evening, handled it badly. My friend Sammy, the one I told you about, who sent me that cable, is fond of quoting an Italian saying to me: "It's easy to travel and change your skies: to change yourself you have to be wise." I think it's about time I made a real effort to change. So there will be no revenge. . . . There's a café about a quarter of a mile along this road and I've been there with my friend du Cros – they'll give us a couple of beers on credit and we can wait there for a lift. Then back to Calvi, showers, and a dinner wherever you choose.'

Bunty sighed: 'Sounds good. Your friend Sammy sounds rather nice too. So wise.'

'He is. Very nice, wise, kind, calm and tolerant. All the mature virtues I lack. But wouldn't have been much use to you on that cliff. He's an acrophobe, has a morbid fear of heights, suffers terribly from vertigo.'

4

Hiss of petrol lamps, flutterings of moths and other faint
night-sounds, a few words of Corse or Italian floating up
to Balfour from another level of the village. Standing
quite still and listening intently he could hear a snatch of
a song, a *serenata* perhaps, and the distant lamenting sigh
of the wind. Perched high in the hills Calenzana had a
mysterious, secretive atmosphere at night, as if it was
conforming to an unknown curfew, and Balfour was
glad that they had stopped there for a drink even though
the glasses of pastis had looked badly smeared.

Instead of waiting for Bunty by the Citroen, he walked
across to the parapet from which they had previously
watched a sunset like a firework display in which each set-
piece eclipsed the one before and in rapid succession the
sky had been painted duck-egg blue, pale violet and
greenish-orange. Now the moon gilded clumps of olive
and fig trees on the statuary hills, and stars flashed enigmatic messages from a vast expanse of gentian sky.

Balfour looked round slowly, trying to imprint on his
mind all that he could see and hear: it was one of those
rare moments when he felt fully alive. The words 'Lost in
the wonder of why we're here' from the song *Dancing in
the Dark* came to him, and he was reminded of how
closely his memories were linked with the world of the
cinema and popular songs. At forty-two he had reached
the stage where people he met for the first time reminded
him of other people he had known and new situations
were very like others he had experienced, but films and
songs gave him an additional background, one which
asserted its existence more often than he would care to

acknowledge. Even on that terrible evening when Barbara had raged at him and they had decided to split up, behind her denunciation he could hear faint overtones of Bette Davis spitting out 'Self, self, self'. Now faced with a beautiful night-sky, he was reminded first of a song and then of the gaiety and insouciance of Ruby Keeler and Dick Powell in an absurd film he had seen when he was about eleven – life at second-hand had as much reality for him as his own. He wondered if this showed an essential triviality in his character, perhaps an emotional incapacity or bankruptcy which led to his 'perpetual immature behaviour'.

The night air was heavy with mimosa but Balfour was aware of another, earthier smell – the odd, pepperish one of *anis*. If you broke the jointed stems you smelt aniseed, but from a distance the plant's aroma was like a mixture of pepper and curry, a quite distinct pungent penetration of the throat and nose, which immediately evoked memories of other holidays he had spent on the Mediterranean.

A few hundred miles away, on Ischia, perhaps looking at this same moonlit sea, Prudence was spending her first holiday away from the family: fast on this thought came the irony of it; he had broken up his family in a cavalier fashion and now he was being sentimental about it. But as he thought of Prudence, her puzzled, guarded yet hurt expression on the day he removed his things from the Orme Square house, Balfour was aware of unaccustomed sensations, an unpleasant one in the throat which made him swallow repeatedly and a pricking at the back of his eyes. He had forgotten that one could really have 'a lump in the throat', and it was so long since he had cried (perhaps thirty years) that it was like a new experience. Tears continued to well up and roll down his cheeks. It seemed that, for some unknown reason, he was at last learning the lesson which Sam Weiss had tried to impress on him some weeks before. Oscar Wilde had written: 'Children begin by loving their parents. After a time they judge them.

Rarely, if ever, do they forgive them.' For a moment he contemplated writing to Prudence and asking her to suspend judgement, then dismissed the impulse – the verdict was in.

'Ned?' Balfour heard his name being called and a rather nervous summoning whistle. He turned to see Bunty standing near a petrol lamp, apparently loath to venture into the shadows of the cobbled lane. He hastened to her, using both hands in a furtive movement to brush the moisture from his face.

'What a weird old place! That man with the mask of blue-black whiskers and the odd tooth or so – he looked just like a bandit. Then when I came out from spending a penny there was an old girl all in black, with skirts down to her ankles, who held my arms and kept trying to tell me something though I couldn't understand a word.'

'It used to be known as the village of gangsters,' Balfour said, 'and I doubt if the police get much co-operation up here even now. I know a few phrases of Corse but it's so clipped that I can't understand anything when they gabble.'

'Oh look!' Bunty bent down at the edge of the lamp's fitful light. 'It's crushed but still alive.'

Balfour crouched beside her and saw a small lizard with its tail and back legs squashed into a groove between two stones. It looked like a heraldic emblem, a miniature dragon caught forever in a position of defiant despair. He examined it carefully and experienced a second's illogical surprise that it should be in a position of such torture without making a sound. No doubt it had been run over by the Citroen when he jockeyed back and forth in parking near the lamp. He gently pushed the girl away and then stamped on the lizard, meeting her protestations with a shrug. 'Nothing else I could do apart from leaving it there to die slowly.'

They got into the car and drove off in silence. They were practically at the bottom of the tortuous twisting hill road when he asked: 'Did you really think I was cruel to do that? In a situation like that what else can you do apart from give the *coup de grâce*? Sammy Weiss, the man I told you about this afternoon, was in a concentration camp before the war and he told me that in there they said that death was a good friend, bringing an end to suffering and pain.'

'Concentration camp *before* the war?'

'Oh yes, they had them then. Sammy's an Austrian Jew but he's also a socialist. The local Nazis must have had a list prepared of people they wanted out of the way because he was arrested on the 15th March 1938, just after Hitler marched into Vienna, and he was in Wollersdorf and Dachau till January 1939. Then his brother arranged for him to be released, and he came to England. But before that he'd been hung in chains. Even now his fingernails. . . . But I'd better not go on. I forget that you weren't even born in '39. Must sound like ancient history to you.'

'It's not that – but it doesn't seem real somehow, I mean possible. Why should a whole nation agree to sadists and lunatics running things – were all the Germans mad at that time?'

'I know what you mean. Even when I first saw newsreels of the camps in 1945 I was trying to find an explanation, make sense of them. In fact I can remember telling a friend that the camps must have been prisons which got out of hand, that the food supplies had run out, that kind of thing. But since the war I've met a dozen or so people who were actually in camps, mostly through Sammy, and now I know a fair amount about them. Too much I think sometimes. Another good friend of mine, Max Weber the art-dealer, ended up in Buchenwald and he's not a Jew – just a Bavarian Catholic who supported the "White Cross" peace movement. Perhaps you can see why it's rather an obsession with me. That's why the telegram from Sammy has me worried – he says that any *häftling*, camp prisoner, had to become independent or he didn't survive. I don't know anyone more independent than him – so how can my advice be "vital" to him?'

'Have you known him long?'

'Since 1952, about as long as I've known Max Weber. I told you I deal in manuscripts and autograph letters; well, Max is a very successful dealer in paintings. At first Sammy was just a customer to both of us – he doesn't have a lot of money to spend but he's extremely knowledgeable and astute in collecting.'

'He wouldn't be wanting your advice before lashing out a particularly large sum?'

'I don't think so. And I'm sure he would not call any decision of that kind "terrible". He has no taste for dramatics. It certainly puzzles me...'

'Why can't you phone him tonight?'

'He's not on the phone at home. He asked me to phone him at the Burlington Arcade where he has a shop, and presumably he wasn't going to be there today. So I must wait.'

'Well, tomorrow you'll probably find you've been worrying unnecessarily. But is there a phone in Calvi? I haven't seen one.'

'Oh yes, two or three booths in the post office.'

Balfour stopped the car, pulling over on to the narrow road's sandy shoulder. He had no faith in the girl's optimistic prophecy, but it was time to stop talking of concentration camps and cables. In the moonlight, with her long straight flaxen hair, she looked touchingly young and beautiful, rather like Tenniel's 'Alice' though this impression was contradicted by her dark grey crew-neck pullover and white cotton trousers.

When they got out of the car he twirled her round by the shoulders so that she had a panoramic view. The old farmhouse known as 'Le Coucou' stood in an isolated spot in the valley of the Bartasca river, a few hundred feet off the road from Calenzana – there were no other buildings within sight and apart from the vines and an occasional cork oak they had an uninterrupted view on every side. The limpid night sky seemed at once immeasurably far off and yet close enough to step into; the air was soft and faintly scented with tamarisk; there was just a slight breeze ruffling the vine leaves, occasionally flashing their silver undersides. Balfour whispered into Bunty's ear: 'They are not long, the days of wine and roses . . .'

She sighed and nodded: 'An evening like this – it's over just in a flash. Simply delicious smells, tamarisk and something herby, rosemary I think.'

'Ah, that's not the *maquis* for once. You can smell the pizzas. They use a lot of herbs. You're sure you wouldn't prefer to go on to the harbour for grilled lobster? It's a very simple meal here with no alternative dishes. Just home-cured ham as a starter, pizza, and their own wine and peaches. And can you do justice to half a yard of pizza?'

'Don't worry too much about that,' Bunty said, pretending to count her fingers. 'Since lunch I've had a long lesson in water-skiing but really the hard way, climbed a cliff covered in *maquis* like barbed wire, hitch-hiked, showered and changed, been taken on hair-raising car trip to the source of a mountain stream, slithered down its dangerous rocks. Yes, I think I can eat my share of a pizza.'

Balfour waved to the proprietress as they went through the white-washed hallway, showing her in pantomime that they were ready for a pizza of the largest possible dimensions. It was a pleasant, simply furnished dining-room, lit only by candles burning in glasses shaped like giant wine goblets throwing arabesques of shadows on the low ceiling. They were watching the *pizzaiolo* busy at his large stove in the corner when they heard British voices in the hall. Balfour thought he recognized the loud, 'county' tones of the male one and Bunty grimaced. '*Sacramento!* My parents. I left a note saying where we were going but didn't expect them to come charging after us. Oh, what a bore!'

When the Hillyards appeared, peering about from the door-way, it seemed from their expressions that they anticipated not being entirely welcome. As they made their way to Balfour's table Mrs Hillyard waved an envelope as if it was an invitation to attend.

'We were just setting off for dinner when we bumped into a chap who had been trying to find you.' Mrs Hillyard handed Balfour the envelope. 'This telegram man seemed to think the message was urgent so we offered to hand it on. Thought we could combine it with one of these celebrated pizzas.'

Balfour thanked her, grinning as if his favourite dinner companions had arrived even though Mr Hillyard's interests in cars, stock exchange, golf and horses were all antipathetic to him. But his disappointment about a spoiled evening was forgotten as soon as the telegram was opened. As he read it he felt as though he had been dealt a stunning physical blow. TRAGIC NEWS SAMMY DIED THIS AFTERNOON IN AN ACCIDENT WRITING BARBARA. He held it before him staring stupidly at the printed words as if he were illiterate, paralysed in an attitude of shock and disbelief.

5

'Sam Weiss?' Mrs Alec Connolly repeated the name thoughtfully but her mind was taken up with other things: she was looking down from the window into Orme Square, idly wondering what the significance of the eagle on the pillar at the front of the square could be, and whether she had asked Barbara about this before; she was also trying to remember who had said 'I spend my life escaping boredom' and if he had left a recipe. While Barbara was in her present impassive, stultifying mood she did not wish to stay, yet there was nothing else she really wanted to do, and there must be six or seven hours to bedtime. She looked surreptitiously at her watch.

'Yes, you know him.' There was a tone of impatience in Barbara Balfour's voice. 'Little man, about five foot six, slight foreign accent, nice kind brown eyes. You met him here. I can remember you two talked about Vienna – the Leopoldstadt area where he lived before the war.'

'Of course. I do indeed remember him. We share an enthusiasm for Schönbrunn. But what about him?'

'I said he was *dead*.'

'Really?'

'It's in here.' Barbara Balfour handed Ruth Connolly a copy of the *Evening Standard* folded in half, pointing to a small paragraph on page ten:

> MAN'S DEATH-DIVE FROM 10TH FLOOR
> A laundry-man fainted on discovering a death-plunge victim at Bowdon Court, Paddington. The man was later identified as Samuel Weiss, a London jeweller . . .

'How awful! Could it be suicide or was it an accident?'
'No idea. It's just bewildering. I knew about it before I

read the papers because the police contacted Ned's office. It seems that Sam had one of Ned's letterheadings in his pocket with the Corsica address scribbled on it. So the police went round and saw Miss Bowyer, Ned's assistant, and she phoned me. I cabled the sad news to Ned and now he's on his way back.'

'So he's giving up the rest of his holiday then?'

'Seems like it. He phoned this morning to say he was booked on a flight reaching London early this afternoon. It's a perfect mystery as Sammy suffered terribly from vertigo. I mean if it was suicide why choose to do it like that? And you couldn't know anyone less neurotic than Sammy.'

'How very sad.' Ruth moved to the window again, looking across to Kensington Gardens, at once puzzled that she felt so little and anxious that the subject should be changed. It was a shock to hear of Mr Weiss's death but she did not want to go on discussing it or brooding on the subject; it was the second death she had heard of in one day and while this one, being an accident, did not really count, it seemed that her generation was now reaching the depressing stage when news of heart attacks and inoperable cancers became fairly frequent. On the other hand time passed by without anything really interesting or exciting developing; she would have to strain her memory to recall any moments of intense pleasure in the past few months; she spent her life waiting for something that never happened. She wanted quite desperately to enjoy herself today. With Barbara generally apathetic and now this depressing accident, the prospect at Orme Square was gloomy indeed. She looked down with a tiny jolt of pleasure at the blackish-green python shoes which had been such a find at Pinet's – they went perfectly with her very light, subtly touched with white, stockings and the new Molyneux dark green silk suit – it really was a rather attractive outfit but it had not aroused any comment from Barbara who would probably only come to life when Toby returned from his tea-party. She thought suddenly, with sharp annoyance, of Alec: no doubt he was enjoying himself all right in San Francisco – he was never bored and perhaps his most irritating habit was flaunting this. Oh God, she thought, you made some of the days too long.

'Where's Toby's party, or did you say?'

'He's playing with the Fielding children. Helga took him but I promised to go at about six and collect. We had, by the way, a delightful little holiday in the Scillies. A real Tiny Tots holiday.'

'How do you mean?'

'Oh, the plane we went in was a biplane, a Dragon Rapide made in 1935, with only six seats for passengers. You felt you could wave to people on the way as it never went out of sight of land. And Toby had a bucket and spade and played in little pools with shrimps and minute green crabs. You see Ned's always dictated holidays before, and Calvi and Praiano aren't really suitable for toddlers.'

Surveying the stream of traffic in the Bayswater Road, Ruth had noticed a taxi pull up by the green gates to the park and a recognizable figure emerge. 'Speaking of Ned,' she said, 'there is a certain would-be Peter Pan figure making his way over here now. Light shining on thinning hair but still a rather bouncy step. There's something about that slightly aggressive gait that reminds me irresistibly of the character, Georgie something or other, in *The Magnificent Ambersons* of whom they all correctly prophesied that he would one day get his come-uppance.'

'Don't be mean,' Barbara replied, 'Ned's probably had his in the last twenty-four hours. Sammy's death will have shaken him very much I know. He was his best friend . . .'

'Don't be *mean*,' Ruth repeated incredulously. 'Really you are an extraordinary girl. After the way he carried on with that silly little piece, and leaving you. I suppose if he says he's feeling down now, you'll say well O.K., move back here then.'

Barbara said nothing and they waited in silence for Balfour to appear. After a few minutes Ruth's face was set in a faintly mischievous smile. 'Perhaps,' she said slowly, 'perhaps he's staying down there trying to get Helga to sympathize about his come-uppance.'

She had barely finished this sentence when Balfour opened the door with an unhappy grin and said hallo in a toneless voice, greeting them both with an offhand wave and slumping down heavily in the rather worn red leather armchair which looked out of place in the otherwise elegant drawing-room. He sighed deeply and rubbed his face as if to get some expression into it. He looked tired in spite of his suntan. His lightweight grey suit was creased and his shoes were dusty. He had shaved badly and cut himself by the cleft in his chin.

'Sorry,' he said vaguely, gesturing with both hands at once as if he might be apologizing for being there, or his appearance, or recent events. 'I feel rather beat, as if I'd been pummelled. You know, when I got your cable I reacted just like a machine being set in motion. Automatically I concentrated on packing up and getting back. Then, in Orly, among all those bloody show-cases, it suddenly hit me. A ghastly sense of anti-climax. What the hell am I doing here I thought? What's the rush? I'd been tearing back as if Sam was desperately ill, as if I could do some good.' He sighed deeply again. 'Have you heard anything about – how it happened?'

'Only this,' Barbara replied, showing him the paper. 'I said in my cable I'd be writing, but all I really know so far is that the police found one of your letter-headings on him and contacted Patricia. She phoned me just to say what had happened, but she knew nothing more.'

'Well, there must be someone who knows what led up to it. I've been going nuts trying to think of a reason, but I simply can't believe he'd kill himself. Well, *you* don't, do you?' he appealed to Barbara.

She shook her head. 'No – but we don't know what the position was.'

Balfour looked at his watch. 'Five-thirty. Pat will have gone by now. I feel a bit strange, slightly wobbly, but then I've only had a cup of coffee since yesterday lunchtime. Your cable was delivered just as I was sitting down to eat a pizza and I scrubbed that. Then there was a mix-up at Nice and I found I hadn't got a booking on the direct flight to London as they promised in Calvi, and as I was supposed to have lunch on that plane I hadn't brought any francs with me, gave them all to Marie-Antoinette. So in Orly I couldn't even buy a beer.'

'Helga can make you some tea.' Barbara suggested in a carefully neutral voice. 'Or you *could* come along to the Fieldings. I've got to pick up Toby. There'll be a drink there and some toothsome tit-bits.'

'No. Thanks, but I'll push on, have a meal ...' The sentence fizzled out as if he had no real plans. 'I'll phone when I have any news about Sammy. I want to come round one day and bring some things I bought for Pru and Toby.'

'I must be going too,' Ruth said quickly. 'And don't offer me a lift, Barbara, as it's right out of your way. I'll get a taxi.'

Balfour and Mrs Alec Connolly descended the stairs in silence. When they emerged from the house she said: 'You might have gone to the Fieldings. Barbara wanted you to.'

Balfour rubbed his patchily stubbled chin. 'Oh, I don't know. I doubt it really. A nice impulsive gesture but making for awkwardness and she'd probably regret it. I don't get on with the Hon. Diana f-ffoulkes-Fielding.'

Ruth Connolly sniffed in irritation. 'You know, your refusal to treat double-barrelled names seriously is just pure inverted snobbery.'

Balfour grinned. 'Shall I bid you adieu right now or may I get you a taxi? I'm usually fairly good at getting taxis.'

At the end of the little square Ruth turned to him: 'Done any other good boasting lately?'

'Howzat?'

She laughed. 'I shall always remember. The absurd way you once went on about "the man in the street's" obsession with sport, prefaced by a catalogue of your own prowess at football.'

'Still true. I retract nothing.'

Taxis sped past continually but they were all full. After his holiday in Corsica Balfour found the continuous stream of traffic in Bayswater Road irritatingly loud, and he looked on the jockeying, lights-racing tactics of the drivers with a hostile eye. Sun shining on the grass and trees in the park made it appear a comparative haven.

Ruth tapped a foot impatiently. 'If we don't get one soon Barbara will appear and feel compelled to offer me a lift, and I'm going in the opposite direction.'

'To Chesterfield Hill?'

'Yes. So?'

'A walk through the Gardens. A peaceful stroll and a better chance of a taxi in the Kensington Road. You'd be half-way home there anyway.' He took her arm but as they crossed the road he felt her move it forward slightly so that it was nearly out of contact. He looked at her but she stared ahead. Before she had always appeared simply indifferent to him, making it quite plain that she was Barbara's friend not his, but this open, faintly silly antagonism was new and he was not sure what it meant. She gave him a quick critical glance as they entered the park gates. 'You're shorter than Alec.'

'That's correct, mam.'

'And his hair hasn't thinned at all.'

'Good for old Alec.'

'Your shoe lace is undone and your suit looks as if you slept in it.'

Balfour laughed. 'Say, this must be stick-a-pin-in-Balfour day and I haven't bought a flag.' He bent down to tie his lace but kept his eye on Ruth as she walked on a few paces. Her flawless legs were shown off perfectly by the rather short dark skirt and seamless pale stockings; she had the perfect, white skin that often goes with titian hair, and suddenly he had a strong desire to see more of it. He made a mock attempt to clean his shoes by rubbing them on the backs of his calves, then brushed his trousers vigorously with his hands. 'There, that's the worst off. And if you've got any scissors on you I can trim these frayed cuffs.'

She smiled faintly and he caught up with her, taking hold of her arm again, rather high up and very firmly. 'Hey! That's a *very* dishy outfit you're wearing.' He turned her round slowly, holding both her arms and inspecting her closely from head to toe. 'Look out. You appear distinctly edible and I'm very hungry. Yes, yew-must-come-along-o'-me, missis. You see! I may be shorter than Alec but I'm a good deal stronger.'

'*Don't* do that.' The command was sharply emphasized but she did not pull her arms away. 'Alec says all that body-building stuff is very suspect. Standing round and admiring your muscles in a mirror.'

'Good old Alec may be right but then I'm not a body builder. Just a creature of habit. You see my parents died when I was five. My father was General Manager of the Bombay Railway and they died in a crash at Baroda. So I was brought up by an aunt who wasn't terribly interested and I didn't spend much time at home. I played a lot of football as you know. And tennis, fives, squash. I took extra gym. I joined the boxing club. I was the last boy to leave the swimming baths in the evening.' He pretended to hook tears delicately from the corners of his eyes with both little fingers and then flick them on to the path. 'This sounds even sadder when I play the violin.'

Ruth gave him a not unsympathetic glance, but before she had a chance to say anything he went on: 'So I got into the habit of doing a lot of swimming. Then again I'm a spare-time navvy – I've helped to build patios and garden-walls from Holyport to Chertsey . . .' He was going to add that he did not expect to receive many other weekend building invitations because they had always come from Barbara's friends, but suppressed this and was struck with another thought –

'You know, at Orly, in a mood of unaccustomed candour I admitted to myself. ... While I was killing time looking in those garish showcases I suddenly caught sight of my own reflection and did glimpse "a selfish expression" – something which Barbara used to accuse me of so often. But don't you think she's unnaturally unselfish? She seems just to want to live for the children. I love them too but – do you know that bit of Chekov? "You must have decent, well-dressed children, and your children, too, must have a nice house and children, and their children again children and nice houses; and what is it all for? The devil knows."'

Ruth shook her head. 'I think anyone can justify anything. Sophistry. Oh damn!' A few large raindrops were spattering the path and there was an ominous black cloud directly above them. Balfour took her hand and they ran towards a shelter. The fanciful, spiring canopy of the Albert Memorial still glittered in the sun and there was a stretch of translucent blue beyond London's bandstand and Kensington Palace, but elsewhere the sky darkened dramatically and rain poured down.

When they reached the hut Balfour glanced covertly at Ruth's face. Impossible to know what she was thinking! But trying to find out would be an interesting pastime and he wanted to prolong the opportunity for study if he could. Her expression was self-contained yet slightly kittenish, reminiscent of Vivien Leigh. She pressed back into the wooden seat under the carved memorial inscription about gallant sailors, but Balfour moved outside again spying a rainbow that straddled the Serpentine. He enjoyed the rain's fresh touch on his face; he felt so grubby that getting damp did not seem to matter much and it took away the last vestiges of weariness. All over the park people were scurrying for cover. Two small boys carrying fishing-nets and jam-jars containing sticklebacks ran up to the shelter, and then scampered off without a word when they saw it was occupied. He watched their haphazard progress to the gate with a slightly rueful expression.

'It's funny. That aunt I told you about. When I was about the age of those kids I was dead set on having a fishing rod – Greenheart, quite a cheap one really. Yearned for it, but didn't get it. So when I first earned some money I always used to carry a spare pound with me so that I could buy that damned rod if I wanted to. Yet now – if today someone was to offer me a free trip to fish the finest river in New Zealand it wouldn't mean a thing.'

The rain was coming fitfully to a stop as the large black cloud moved away, with a few last drops being shaken down as if someone was reluctant for the display to stop. Balfour realized that he was not altogether pleased that it was ending. The sun sparkled on the spray from the fountains and glistened on the giant equestrian statue by the Round Pond. Balfour pointed to it: 'Everything's had a wash and brush up except me.'

Ruth got up and stood by his side with a teasing secretive smile. She was so close that her gardenia scent was heady.

'Well – if you don't want that old fishing rod what would you like?'

'Mmmm.' He put his left arm round her waist and looked straight into her eyes as he pondered this question, watching her closely to detect the subtlest response to his reply. 'What do I want? First a wash. Then two or three inches of pure malt whisky, preferably Talisher's. . . . Then something to eat with plenty of red wine, and then . . .' His left hand moulded her hip-bone and his fingers strayed over into the soft curve below.

'What a brutish programme!'

Balfour shrugged, ready to abandon the idea. 'Well, that's what I'd like.'

Her pointed nails closed round his left wrist like a trap. 'Where can you buy this Talisher stuff?'

6

'Guilty!' Balfour started up in a cold sweat from a vivid and humiliating dream. The verdict boomed and echoed in his ears. In the dream he had been searching through a large Victorian house which looked as though it had been shut up for years with sunlight coming through heavily dust-marked windows, and the stale-smelling rooms full of grimy furniture which had to be moved around laboriously for him even to advance a little way from the doors. The stuffiness was enervating and it seemed as if the supply of air was gradually being exhausted. When he had reached the top floor the search became more urgent, though he had still not understood its purpose. Opening a series of attic doors he found it was now twilight and the gloomy small rooms there were cold and damp. Then he heard a hurdy-gurdy grinding out a waltz and clambered up on a chair to one of the tiny awkward windows to look with difficulty down on a group of men, women and children being shepherded along a narrow street: as he stared down Max Weber and Sam Weiss looked up and waved gaily, shouting some words he could not hear. From his vantage point he alone could see that at the end of the street a train composed of closed goods wagons waited for them. He had rushed down the stairs as the music changed to that of a military band with loudly clashing cymbals playing at an increasing tempo. In a panic, unable to think, he had charged with his shoulder at the locked front door to find that it opened into a small, crowded court-room with someone calling out in a dead-sounding voice *'Wieviel stück?'* over and over again, despite the answering repetition '650 pieces in 12 goods wagons'. Then he was pushed through the crowd and confronted by a young girl with long blonde hair covering her face, obviously nude apart from a shabby overcoat much too large for her. He was aware without being told that he would be found innocent of his unknown crime if he did not touch her but with a feeling of fascination and horror he had embraced her, tugging the clumsy cloth away from her peerless bare shoulders, hearing at once the echoing verdict and the train slowly chugging out of the station.

Balfour could feel the pricking sensation of tiny drops of sweat on his scalp. Once before he had experienced a similar nightmare, another unnerving elaboration of guilt, some days after he had been with Sam to see a haunting film about the war-time ghetto in Warsaw. He sprang out of bed and had a cold shower, feeling that the grime and cobwebs of the old house had to be literally scrubbed away.

When he shaved he saw how vividly his scars stood out now that he was so deeply tanned. It was ironic that most wartime scars were a testimony to the victim's efforts to end the Nazi horror, but his reminded him only of the futility of his five weeks in Italy – and that while train-loads of Jews were being butchered he had been playing football for Eastern Command, when old ladies and children were being marshalled with knouts and Alsatian dogs he had been grumbling about conditions at Catterick and Aldershot Barracks.

He shaved quickly but much more efficiently than he had done the previous morning in Calvi, then put on a kettle to make some Nescafé Continental. The refrigerator was turned off and bare apart from one lemon in the egg-shelf, but he did not feel like going out for breakfast. He put some sultanas in a fruit plate and moistened them with lemon juice, and took his meagre meal into the spacious living-room, furnished with only two red leather armchairs and a couch.

Some of Balfour's friends had criticized his flat in Bury

Street: the large white block was 'clinical', 'cold-looking', 'impersonal'. This did not worry him and he had continued the effect by having all his rooms painted white, laying dark blue carpet throughout, and putting in the absolute minimum amount of furniture. Years of seeing other people's possessions being dispersed at auction sales had left him with a strong feeling against making such an accumulation for himself. A worn edition of Sir Thomas Browne was the only book he kept; otherwise he read paperbacks, giving them away as soon as they were finished. A reproduction of Vermeer's *Head of a Girl* was the sole wall decoration.

Music was important in Balfour's life, and a small collection of records in a stainless steel rack was an exception to his prejudice against possessions. He sat on the slate-blue linen couch and listened to Billie Holiday singing *Loveless Love* while he drank his coffee and ate the sultana substitute for *muesli* which was his usual breakfast. Afterwards he put on one of Sam Weiss's favourite jazz discs, the Art Tatum-Ben Webster Quartet playing *Night and Day*, and fetched some more coffee, a calendar and a sheet of paper from the kitchen. At the top of the blank page he wrote 8th July, the last day on which he had seen Sammy: at the bottom he put 1st August, the day that S. had died.

He had good reason to remember the evening of the 8th July and knew that Sammy had been his normal positive and lively self then. They had first tracked down an old W. C. Fields film and then dined at Bloom's in Whitechapel High Street on beetroot bortsch and stuffed kishka. Coming back to Bury Street, they had settled down to coffee and listening to Brahms and Beethoven. It was during the adagio of the F Major quartet that Sammy had said enigmatically, with a hint of accusation, 'Beethoven's thoughts on death', giving a funny look as though Balfour should find this particularly salutary.

When the record was finished Sammy had said with a sigh, 'Yes, life is so short,' and then launched into a lecture on Balfour's behaviour, telling him bluntly that he should not have left Barbara: 'The children matter most. You don't like your life with her, well you must lump it. Put up with it. Forget what *you* want for a bit and think about Toby and Prudence.'

There was no one else who would have dared to talk to Balfour like that and certainly no-one to whom he would have listened. He had sat there silent with growing irritation. (How easy to pinpoint other people's stupidities; how facile to suggest solutions for their problems: as simple and ineffective as saying abracadabra.) His obvious though silent hostility had finally provoked Sammy into saying bitter things about people who refused to grow up and face up to their responsibilities, then leaving in an awkward silence. Neither of them had made any effort to get in touch before Balfour had left for Corsica on the 15th July.

He looked at the calendar again. How odd it was to think that in those three weeks Sammy had been caught up in events that led to his violent death. Samuel Jacob Weiss, 'a Jew by birth, an infidel by temperament', born on the 2nd February, 1911, in a small house in Schiffamt-gasse in the Leopoldstadt, the Viennese equivalent of London's East End, imprisoned in Dachau in 1938, exiled in 1939, was dead. Lover of children and music, humanist, socialist, connoisseur of jewels, manuscripts and paintings – what meaning did his life have now that it was ended? His body was presumably in a hospital mortuary and soon would be finally disposed of at the Golders Green Crematorium – like Balfour, Weiss had no religious beliefs and only rarely, reluctantly, had attended the Liberal Jewish synagogue in St John's Wood to please his elderly sister who had subsequently gone to live in Tel Aviv. Looking at the newspaper account of the 'death-plunge victim' Balfour said '*Meschugge*' as it seemed a more apt comment than any English phrase. A Hebrew word which had survived in Yiddish, it meant 'mad' but carried the additional idea of an empty, melancholic, lunar folly.

Balfour opened a window wide and looked out towards Pall Mall. A slight breeze moved the curtains and the morning air was unused, temptingly fresh. There had been more rain during the night and an electric milk van slid noiselessly over asphalt which was drying patchily with the damp showing in grotesque patterns. The sky was a watery blue and the sunlight feebly warm after the fierce glare he had been used to in Corsica. It was just the kind of day he liked for walking round London, and he was glad that he was not committed to sitting it out in Sotheby's or Christie's. He decided to call in at his office and then go round to Carlos Place for a talk with Max Weber.

*

As Balfour turned the corner into Jermyn Street he nearly bumped into a girl with abundant lively red hair and eyes of the same rare light brown colour as Mrs Alec Connolly's. The evening with Ruth had been an instructive one. It was not the first time that he had found an apparent indifference masked a physical attraction, but he had not known another woman so frank about her desires and forthright in her language. At one crucial point her bluntness had led first to giggling and then to mutual laughter which had nearly the opposite effect to that she intended. Even so, his pulse raced at the memory of her slim hands urgently caressing his shoulders and then her nails lightly digging into the back of his neck, holding him tight to her white full-breasted body. Her languorous sighs – the final deep, drugging kisses.

Afterwards, when he had asked her why she had agreed to his programme for the evening, her answer had been typically direct and unflattering. She had told him there was a *gelataria* in Florence that sold particularly delicious ices and was cunningly named *'Perchè no'*.

'Why not?' – he had met his match in Mrs Alec Connolly. It was the same 'living for pleasure' attitude, a desire to gratify random impulses, which Sam Weiss had attacked so bitterly. Balfour could find no defence for it himself, but then his feelings towards women led him into a labyrinth of motives and desires which he could not disentangle.

Balfour's office in Jermyn Street was near London's finest cheese shop. On the third floor and with only a very small brass plate 'T. EDWARD BALFOUR. MANUSCRIPTS & AUTOGRAPH LETTERS', by the front door, it did not attract any 'passing trade', but he wanted only callers who were seriously interested in his wares and would search him out. When he had first taken the office his assistant, Patricia Bowyer, had displayed a few framed facsimiles of famous letters in the hall but two of them, though worthless, had been stolen and he had scrapped the idea. Now there was nothing to tempt the passer-by to mount the stone steps. The hallway was painted an unattractive shade of brown which had been accurately described in a coarse phrase by 'Chas.' Squibb, but Balfour had not even attempted to persuade his landlord to change this.

When he opened the door of the show-room his typist Jane Lupton was bent over a cleared desk moving pieces of an old parchment document about as though it was a jigsaw puzzle. She said hallo quietly, with a sad little smile of sympathy, and he just waved an acknowledgement before going through to a larger room which he shared with Miss Bowyer. Patricia Bowyer was typing but she pulled the paper from the machine on seeing him and balled it up. She seldom expressed her feelings and he was surprised to see her visibly disturbed. Squeezing the paper ball mechanically she said: 'Oh dear. This was a letter to you. We were terribly sorry to hear about Mr Weiss. But you know how Jane and I liked him. Such a horrible shock!'

There was a momentary quiver of her lips and Balfour was aware that she was precariously balanced on the edge of tears – the muscles of her throat moved in stiff little swallows. He had never seen her like this before and he felt at a loss for words. He remembered now that she and

Sam had occasionally popped out for coffee together — they had a mutual, passionate interest in music.

'Masses of notes here. I was just writing to you about some of them.' Her voice was firmer, more in control. He moved near to her desk. There were two pages of quarto typing paper in front of her. One was covered with a large number of her usual neat notes. Those on the other page were nervously scrawled and appeared elliptical.

Patricia waved him away from this page. 'I shall have to translate this. Monday, 1st August, Detective Sergeant Lowther called in here.' She peered doubtfully. 'Four-thirty p.m. From D Division, Harrow Road Police Station, Paddington. Told me what had happened, and that ...' She faltered and again her voice became uncertain. 'That Mr Weiss had a telegraph form in his pocket with a draft of a cable to you. Apparently he'd spoiled it. And he had one of our letterheads which I had given him with your Calvi address. I told him you would be away a week and that I would see you were informed. ... He said that someone from Mr Weiss's shop had identified. ... Then yesterday a Detective Superintendent Hanson from Scotland Yard phoned. He said he was looking into this as "D Division is rather tied up just now". Apparently he had been told at De Jong's that you were Mr Weiss's best friend and his executor. He said the body had been taken to the Westminster Mortuary, Horseferry Road, London, s.w.1., and was now under the jurisdiction of the coroner and could not be removed from there without the coroner's permission. There would be a post mortem and probably an inquest. I told him you would be returning from Calvi at the end of this week and he asked that I contact him as soon as possible.' She paused and looked through her notes again, then shook her head. 'That's all.'

Balfour sat on the edge of his desk. 'Thanks. I'm very sorry you've had to deal with this. Will you phone him this morning and say I can call round this afternoon or any time tomorrow? In a few minutes I want to pop out and see Mr Weber.'

Patricia Bowyer nodded and put the other page of notes in his hand. 'These are business – mostly straightforward. Perhaps I should amplify one. Miss Phelips phoned on 22nd July – said she had forgotten you were away. I thought – I may be wrong – that she sounded slightly put out ...'

'That's odd.' Balfour did not doubt that Patricia had judged Miss Phelips' tone correctly – he had great faith in her perceptiveness and was always ready to take the warning implied in her rare sudden harsh laugh, which was her method of attacking someone's probity.

Miss Olivia Malise Phelips was far and away Balfour's best customer. A woman of great wealth, she lived comparatively simply in the rambling Malise house in Roehampton, administering trusts and charities, reading omnivorously, growing roses and peaches. She collected poetical manuscripts with the intention that they should eventually go to the Bodleian Library, and it was on her behalf that Balfour made most of his flying visits to New York and Paris. In buying for her he was allowed to use his own discretion, and her account was paid invariably on the first of the month. But their relationship had long since ceased to be a purely commercial one. He looked forward keenly to visits to her house and to hearing her quiet, ironic comments on life. On two delightful occasions he had taken her in his car to see the ruins that remained of the Phelips' mansion, Crabbe's Park, near Malmesbury. Their tastes were very similar and the difference in their ages seemed unimportant when he was in her company – he always felt he was talking to a contemporary rather than a woman who had been born in 1890. In his time he had lost several customers due to his impatience and impulsiveness, and usually he preferred that Patricia Bowyer should deal with collectors while he concentrated on buying, but Miss Phelips was an exception to this rule and even a suggestion that she was annoyed was rather disturbing.

'You did tell her you would be abroad?' Patricia queried.

'Of course. And I checked with her that there was nothing she wanted at the London sales while I was away.'

'Perhaps she remembered that when I told her and didn't like to admit it. She is getting on and does forget things sometimes.'

'She might – she might,' Balfour murmured doubtfully.

'Oh, one final thing. Mr Garratt has moved again.' Patricia's voice was deliberately flat as if she was suppressing any comment. She picked up a big, deckle-edged card, looked at it for a moment then handed it to Balfour. Her tone became a little tart: 'From the Quadrant Arcade to Dover Street. To Wigmore Street. To Crawford Street. And now to Lampeter Parade – it's next to a greengrocer's.'

The card was set in a large italic type and decorated with an engraving of an eighteenth-century popinjay removing his hat and bowing. 'Mr Howard St John Garratt begs leave to announce the removal of the Quadrant Galleries to larger premises in Lampeter Parade, W.C.2. Telephone number to be announced later.' The printing was amateurish and uneven. Balfour stared at the card, pondering if there was indeed something about it, and the uncertain telephone status, which would raise doubts in a recipient's mind of Garratt's financial position, or if it was just his own hard-won knowledge. 'Poor old Howard. This must have been sudden.'

Patricia said, 'A moonlight flit I should think.'

Balfour pocketed the card. 'I'll need this. I must call on Howard after Max. One of them should have seen Sam in the last week or so.'

7

Our life is short and our days run
As fast away as does the sun

Balfour made his way from Jermyn Street along Piccadilly and Berkeley Street to the insistent rhythm of the
lines by Herrick which were engraved on the old sun-dial
in Olivia Phelips' garden at Roehampton. They went
round and round in his head without any depressing
effect – indeed, they heightened his physical pleasure in
being alive and feeling the sun's rather meagre warmth
upon his back. It was a cloudy day with pallid sunshine
and a feeling more of autumn than summer, but it was
perfect for strolling about the metropolis. Balfour kept
his Lancia in a lock-up garage in Hendon and rarely used
it in London. Occasionally he would take a taxi or bus,
but he preferred to walk. During twenty years he had
quartered London on foot and had found innumerable
odd places which interested him – a street behind the
Portobello Market which tough-looking gypsies used for
selling suspect cars, the bizarre mixture of tombs and gas-
works at Kensal Green, the melancholy decaying tene-
ments of Columbia Square, Shad Thames.

While he was looking around him, noting a furtive expression on a doorman's face, the eroded 'Nymph' statue
by Munro, and the superb flowers in Moyses Stevens in
Berkeley Square, another part of his mind was occupied
with a memory which just could not be hauled up into
the light. Its shadowy form had teased him since he had
been talking with Patricia Bowyer. Then, suddenly, as he
walked past Bruton Street, from its immense rag-bag re-
pertory his mind pulled out the fragment. Quite clearly he
heard a voice from the past. It was Sammy telling him
how his brother Dr David Weiss had died: 'A hopeless

form of cancer. Melanosis – an abnormal deposit of black pigment. Nothing could be done ...' It was perhaps ten years since David Weiss had died, and Balfour was not conscious of thinking of it since. Was that possibly a clue to Sammy's own death? Had he been informed that he too had cancer and needed an urgent operation? This might account for the cable 'VITAL I HAVE YOUR ADVICE ON TERRIBLE DECISION. ...' Even so he could not believe that Sammy would not face up to such an operation. Engrossed in this problem, he went through the stream of traffic from Mount Street oblivious of his surroundings and pulled up just as he was walking past the steps to Max Weber's house.

A casual passer-by would have had no idea that he was only a few steps from one of the finest small art galleries in London. On the corner of Carlos Place, facing the Connaught Hotel, it was indistinguishable in a row of similarly pleasant looking red brick houses. The white number on glass panes above the front door was five inches high, but the name MAX WEBER LTD FINE ART was in tiny gold letters on a small marble plaque requiring abnormal eyesight to read it from the street, and even as one mounted the steps it was difficult to see any paintings in the shadowy room behind the window box.

The weight of the Padauk door might have been the first sign to the perceptive caller that this was a rather special house. Then there was a small hall containing on the left hand wall a fine example of lapidary art, the motto

THE WAY OF FREEDOM
IS OF LIMITATION
LET EACH MAN TAKE
UP HIS CHISEL AND
INSCRIBE HIS OWN FATE

cut on a panel of Hopton-Wood stone, and on the right a charmingly coloured Catazala majolica reproduction of the Madonna and Child by della Robbia, which was of little value and not for sale.

Balfour carefully opened the interior door of ebony and bronze fleur-de-lys grille work and entered the first showroom on the right. It was empty and his attention was taken up by a striking painting of a little girl with large brown eyes and delicately curved lips.

There were quiet footsteps on the saffron carpet and Oliver Gerrard, Weber's chief assistant, appeared. He smiled, showing teeth suitable for a dentrifrice advertisement, but Balfour thought he detected a hint of deep boredom.

Gerrard was the main obstacle between entering the house and going upstairs to see Max. Habitually dressed in a dark grey suit, cream shantung shirt and black tie, always slightly tanned and with perfectly barbered short black hair, Gerrard first hovered discreetly, then politely questioned callers. Anyone who had looked in thinking that 'Fine Art' implied reproductions or that he might find a bargain for a few pounds was soon shepherded back through the hall. Gerrard also dealt with most of the more serious inquiries. He had an encyclopedic knowledge of art – Max had once pointed to the monumental Nonnemacher's *History of Art* saying, 'I don't need that with Oliver around' – and only a handful of customers actually got to see Mr Max Weber at Carlos Place. Over a period of years Gerrard had asked Balfour random questions on literary subjects, knowing it was useless to talk to him about paintings, and having found Balfour's knowledge was often sketchy he now confined himself to generalities. He was always superficially friendly, but nevertheless managed to convey his surprise that Max should want to bother with seeing Balfour.

'Cornelius de Vos.' Gerrard came closer, with a discreet whiff of West Indian Lime cologne, indicating some quality of the painting with a sternly controlled gesture. His enthusiasm escaped in the way he regarded it, saying,

'Very like the subject of his "Little Girl with a Bell".'
Then he took a step back and said, 'My, what a tan!'

Gerrard took two holidays a year in Sicily and was the
last person to be impressed by sun-tan. Balfour did not
like to hear the palpably false compliment for he knew
Gerrard's gift for saying what he judged would be welcome.

Balfour saw Elizabeth Savoyent in the hall – a tall, remote Viennese girl whom he found more intimidating
than Gerrard. He was struck again by the fact that all of
Max's assistants were of a pattern: quiet, discreet, very
polite and, underneath, as tough as old boots. Max's
motto was 'Befehl ist Befehl', and Balfour thought that
being employed by him must be like walking an unending
tightrope, but if one could always obey orders efficiently
then undoubtedly the rewards would be high. He knew
that Gerrard had a house in Seymour Street and a cottage
in Palermo.

There was some mute communication between Gerrard and Miss Savoyent, who said: 'You wanted to see Mr
Weber? I'll go up. He has someone with him at the
moment.'

When she had gone Gerrard grinned and seemed to
relax. For a moment Balfour glimpsed another, carefully
suppressed, personality. 'Someone is an understatement.
There's five hundred pounds of prime Texas beef on the
hoof upstairs.' It was a rare confidence, made under the
pressure of unusual irritation and Balfour guessed its
source: 'Not Mr Henry Beutel Temple II?'

'The same. And his old Mum!' Gerrard raised his eyes
heavenwards in a faintly pansyish expression of despair.

The Beutel Temples visited Europe twice a year, always sending selected dealers a printed circular letter,
'Mother and I will be over again,' listing dates of their
'usual tight schedule' when they would be at Brown's
Hotel in London, the Amstel in Amsterdam, Maurice in
Paris, and Bar au Lac in Zurich. They collected manuscripts as well as paintings, and it was with great satisfac-

tion that Balfour had noticed their London trip dates were safely within the period he was due to be away. His unforeseen return had changed things.

He tugged at his ear with a thoughtful expression. 'Perhaps I won't bother Max just now.'

'You will, you know. You'll go straight on up like a good boy.'

Hearing the attractive 'little girl' voice, Balfour looked round and saw Mrs Max Weber on the curve of the staircase.

'Phyl – how nice!'

She put out both hands as she came down, then proferred her cheek for him to kiss. As he did so he was shocked by a dramatic change in her appearance. Her skin was an unhealthy junket-white, her cheek dry and her hands hot. Her mouth was slightly open and he could smell gin.

She covered her face with her hands in an uncertain movement. 'You mustn't look too close. I'm only just out of bed. No face on yet.' She looked quite ill and her gaiety was forced, like a mockery of her usual gamine self. 'I feel I'm just off the boat.' She laughed nervously. 'Or still on the plane anyway. We've had the four most hectic days in Switzerland. You know Max the human dynamo! I think I've left bits of me in various galleries and apartments – if I can just have a quiet half-hour then they'll come together again, I hope ...'

She paused and impulsively reached out for Balfour's right hand again, holding the tips of his fingers tightly. 'Oh God! All that chat and I haven't said a word about Sammy. We were *so* depressed to read about it. Horrible! Just the cold bare announcement in print. "Later identified ..." Poor old Ned, you must be down. I know Max wants to see you about it. He was quite appalled and baffled – but I don't expect you understand it either. I know he feels guilty about being away too. Apparently Sam came round here the morning. ... Well, the very morning. What a stupid world!'

She talked rapidly and as if her mind was not on what she was saying, moving round in an inconsequential way. Her eyes which Balfour had often thought looked like glittering topazes were now quite dull. She wore brown Gucci shoes, hallmarked by the miniature stirrups linked across the vamp, a dark brown velvet skirt and a pink Hermes blouse with exotic printed feathers; but the attractive clothes seemed to have been slung on without any care, her stockings were wrinkled and her short chestnut hair looked as if it had not been touched since the previous night.

She whispered confidentially: 'You've heard we have the Beutel Temples here. That's always enough by itself to put Max on edge. You know how they dither and waste time. And then that terrible aura of embarrassment they carry around with them. *Do* be conciliatory, dear boy.' She seemed already to have forgotten Sam's death; Max's desires were paramount with her as always.

Balfour nodded. 'I shall be a study in conciliation.'

He walked up the elegant staircase slowly, looking at the figured Indian laurel panels on the walls. Usually he was whisked up and down by Miss Savoyent who did not allow any dawdling. Max's door was open and as he approached he heard Max say 'a putative ascription' in a chilly voice which did not welcome further comment. When he went through the door he was immediately struck by the similarity of the Beutel Temples, looking just like Tweedledom and Tweedledee, turning to regard him with blank sagacious faces. Phyl Weber had not exaggerated their strange talent for spreading embarrassment. Entering the room was like being involved in a scene from an early talking film, circa 1930, when one was very conscious of silence and every sound, every clink of a coffee-spoon, was exaggerated; the occupants all seemed on edge and self-conscious. Balfour immediately had the impression that he was guilty of some unforgivable solecism.

'I saw Phyl – she said I should come up.'

'Of course.' Max smiled and then grimaced sadly, his cardplayer face showing an unusual amount of emotion.

Mr Henry Beutel Temple said, 'Well, hello *Ned!*' forcefully but without enthusiasm, and Max's expression again became remote and defensive.

The Temples were both seated facing Max, so Balfour took a little chair by Max's black walnut desk. It was a large attractive room with a deep golden carpet, heavy cream and gold wallpaper and striped terracotta curtains with huge swags and bobbles. There was one painting on view: a masterpiece by Gerard Van Spaendonck, a basket of flowers on a marble ledge beside an alabaster urn. On a black walnut table by the wall there was an Atmos clock by Jaeger-LeCoultre, a framed photograph of Kennedy and Khrushchev seated on a couch, and crisp unopened copies of *Die Welt, Algemeen Handelsblad, Neue Zürcher Zeitung* and *The Times*.

Max's hair was thin but it was so skilfully cut at Trumper's that this was not very noticeable. He had a long straight nose with a high bridge and heavily developed brow; there were prominent tendons in his cheeks and his mouth was drawn down at the corners as though from pain or irritability. His face was as calm as Buster Keaton's, but restlessness, impatience, unfulfilled desires showed in his blue-grey eyes.

'No,' he said, shaking his head, 'I shouldn't put unbounded faith in what "Tony" Suffolk says. For Italian seventeenth century Mr Denis Mahon is the expert,' he concluded firmly.

Mrs Beutel Temple leant forward towards Balfour and said in a stage whisper: 'We were at Jermyn Street last week and were so sorry to miss you. But we had a nice little visit with Miss Patricia and she showed us some of the goodies in back. We bought some fine things.' The sentence ended with a short blink of her staring eyes and once again she looked like a grotesquely fat doll. The Beutel Temples in the presence of Max Weber were on their best behaviour; it was obvious that there would be

61

none of their usual malicious rumours and cunningly snide remarks.

Max looked up at this, smiling at Balfour: 'I always say that Ned has a quite unique talent for finding things. He should be called "The Nose". I remember a good friend of mine, in this very room, casually mentioning in front of us both that he was particularly interested in a story by Thomas Mann. Some youthful indiscretion, a tale of incest by the Master which was to have appeared in a magazine but was suppressed by his family. Within two weeks he was the astounded owner of both the manuscript and proof. Ned had found it – where? – wasn't it mouldering in some printer's cellar?' A certain mild facetiousness off-set the compliment. His tone subtly implied a little contempt for anyone so footloose and impulsive as to embark on what would probably be a wild goose-chase across Europe for a story of incest.

The Beutel Temples both had an owlish look and made no comment. Max gave the matter a long considering slant of his large head. He seemed to have retreated to some coign of advantage, remote, unreachable.

The awkward silence was broken by the nearly silent entrance of Miss Savoyent: *'Da ist ein Telefonanruf von Herr Cato. Möchten Sie es nehmen? Hier?'*

Max replied: *'Ja bitte, verbinden Sie ihn!'* It was obvious to Balfour that the Temples, like himself, had some knowledge of German – there was a slight change in their expressions. They were at once alert, anticipating hearing a tale to add to their vast repertoire. Mr L. K. G. Cato, head of the great exporting firm, Toller, Cato, was reputed to be one of the few British collectors of paintings who were in their own class, perhaps even above it.

Max usually sounded sharp and distrustful on the phone as if he expected to be tricked, but his 'Leonard-*Willkommen!* I found a little treasure for you' simply expressed pleasure and friendship. He went on to make some small talk about his trip to Switzerland which must have irritated the Temples as it gave nothing away, but

Balfour was glad to have a chance to covertly study Max's face. The immobility of the lower part was due to plastic surgery which had skilfully covered up damage done by an SS man's truncheon in 1945, but he could also mask his eyes so that it was impossible to know what he was thinking. At auction sales no one had any idea whether he was pleased or dissatisfied by the way the bidding went.

When Max's telephone conversation was finished he turned to Mrs Beutel Temple: 'Oh, I nearly forgot, Olga. When you're in Zurich do call in on Mannheimer. He has a fine group of Louis Breguet watches – from the Salomons collection ...' He broke off to explain to Balfour: 'Superb timepieces which were very much in demand in the Napoleonic era, showing the day of the week, phases of the moon, etcetera. Wellington had one.' Max frowned thoughtfully then yawned, partly disguising this with a restless movement. The Temples realized somehow that their palaver was finished. They got up slowly from their chairs and Mr Temple shook Balfour's hand with persistence though he looked as if he did not enjoy doing it. It took a long time for them to go even with the expert guiding of Miss Savoyent, and Max rolled his eyes.

When their loud braying voices could no longer be heard he said: 'At last. Sorry about that. We just got back last night and we only read about Sammy in the plane. Do you know what really happened?'

'No. No idea. That's why I called round – I didn't know you were abroad too!'

'Oh, purely a business trip. Just four days whizzing round to see people. ... How could a thing like that happen? What kind of place was it?'

'I'm sorry, Max. I can't tell you anything. Later on – I have to see the police – when I know the details I'll contact you again. At the moment I can't even begin to guess.'

Max sighed deeply. 'I wonder if he could have got into some kind of mess.'

Balfour shook his head doubtfully. 'I can't think of anything. He seemed fine when I last saw him. And financially ...'

Max made a brief waving movement of dismissal. 'No. For cash he could have come to you, or I would have backed him. But there are other pitfalls. One hears strange things about people one knows. Terrible things.'

Balfour watched Max's expression closely – there was a darkness there – was it anger, fear?

'And they can happen so suddenly. I'll tell you a story, ugly but true, that I heard only the other day.' Max looked down at his immaculate nails with distaste. 'I have a very wealthy customer. Swiss. Lives in Zurich but he has a country "shack" right on Lake Geneva between Lausanne and Vevey. Collects Dutch seventeenth century. Has wonderful paintings by Bol and Dou and Flinck. A gentle old man of great taste and sensitivity. Well, so the old man has a young, flighty wife. She has even ...'

Max shook his head wearily and his eyes looked desperate for a moment. 'From their country place they went to a party at Villars and returned very late, all a little drunk, in their big Mercedes. My old friend sat at the front with the chauffeur. His wife and a "friend" sat at the back. There was some playful nonsense going on in the back seat. Giggling, feeble protests, that kind of thing. The old man ignored this. Then silence at the back. Think of that, Ned, the absorbed, the horrid silence. At last the old man has to turn round and finds the two of them – joined together. The "friend" is immersed in his wife's parts. ... Regardless of the risk, like rutting animals. No, insects – that's better. Have you ever seen dragonflies in sexual congress, curved together in a taut circle? You could go right up to them as they hang entwined from a twig, dash them to the ground if you would. So this gentle old man found himself reaching over into the back of the car trying to part these fornicating insects. Then there was some kind of disgusting drunken scuffle with the chauffeur involved too. Do you think that when the old man shaved that morning, looking out over Lake

Geneva, he ever dreamed that within a few hours. . . .
You see. Such things can happen quickly. They "boil up",
get out of control . . .' He shook his head again in eloquent
inarticulateness. Cool smoke-blue light glittered in his
eyes.

For Balfour there was some unreality about the story –
at some point it had been exaggerated, either in the old
man's mind crazed with jealousy, or possibly in Max's distaste for sex.

Suddenly Max got up and walked over to touch the pile
of unopened papers on the walnut table. 'Do let me know
what you find about Sam. And you must come to dinner
soon. I've recently acquired some *Hattenheimer Nub-
brunnen Riesling* – a *trockenbeerenauslese* of quite
superb quality. Come and help us drink a bottle. Phyl
would like that too.'

Max smiled and put his hand on Balfour's arm – a rare
gesture of friendship, but also one of dismissal because
secretly a bell must have been rung. Miss Savoyent appeared silently and in a few moments Balfour was once
again glancing at the della Robbia majolica plaque on his
way out of the house.

8

'Go on, piss off' was Balfour's vocal introduction to Lampeter Parade. Stepping out of an alley-way in the Seven Dials area between Cambridge Circus and Covent Garden he at once noticed the Parade's nameplate on a wall and heard this forthright advice. Glancing along to his left he saw four small scruffy carts, uniformly painted white and decorated with a pig enjoying a sausage and the motto 'GALLEY'S HOT DOGS ARE THE PORKIEST'. A further look at the absorbed group of unkempt youths about the carts was enough to assure him that he had not been so peremptorily addressed. He walked past them slowly, noting the chipped paint, greasy washing-up bowls and grey cloths, wondering how they escaped the attention of the Public Health Department and managed to sell their wares.

It was an appropriate introduction to the Parade, the first part of which consisted of a high grimy brick wall, topped with broken glass and posted with No Admittance signs. Then there was a row of bleak shops dating from the Victorian era, all with disproportionately high doorways and an air of being deserted though most of them were ostensibly open for business.

Garratt's shop-door was shut and the black lettering of 'Quadrant Galleries' on the cream façade was only half finished. In the window there was a chair, a step-ladder, a pot of paint and a 'closed' notice. Hanging on the door a Donald Duck cardboard clock proclaimed that the shop would be open, surprisingly enough, at half-past six. Balfour pushed at the door and it swung back.

The dim interior was full of open crates, cardboard

cartons, paintings and empty frames. It had a very high ceiling and would look exceedingly depressing in artificial light. The back of the shop was partitioned off by the two large *art nouveau* screens of which Garratt was inordinately proud.

Slowly Balfour became aware of odd noises behind the screens – heavy breathing, muffled shouts, the sound of things being knocked down. He walked quickly to the side of the largest screen and saw Howard St John Garratt scuffling with an equally small red-haired man. Garratt wore an out-moded sports jacket with golf ball buttons, an Etonian tie, jeans and dirty co-respondent shoes. The cumbersome paraphernalia of a National Health hearing aid still hung from his ear though he looked very dusty, as if he had been dragged along the floor a few times. Balfour interposed himself between the couple, holding them off easily. They were well matched, both game but slight. Garratt's arm felt touchingly thin. He claimed (and most of his unlikely stories turned out to be true) that he had been to both Eton and Harrow, and Balfour had often been puzzled how an upbringing which included periods at the best public schools could have produced such a puny rachitic physique.

The ginger-headed man in frustrated rage had gone beyond heavy breathing and was making a noise like a child who has sobbed past exhaustion. After a minute, pointing a nicotine-stained finger at Garratt, he managed to say, 'Never mind. I'll have yew – yew'll see.'

Garratt replied enigmatically, 'Well, that's that then,' opening wide his prominent hazel eyes in what he no doubt considered a challenging look.

Balfour felt extraordinarily sane and well-balanced, as he always did in Garratt's company. When he said 'What's all this about?' he realized that he sounded just like a policeman.

The irascible red-haired man's voice became even more strident: 'I'll tell yew what the —ing trouble's about. This —er has had some pricey stuff from me. Best —ing

67

strip lighting, switches, spot lamps. Now he's given me a kite. —ing cheque came back this morning. N.B.G. Little twister!'

Garratt had drawn away from Balfour's restraining hand and was once more in control of the situation. His head was cocked at a knowing angle and his voice took on a superior tone. 'But I've told this – chap that it's a purely temporary thing. Just a brief withdrawal of the bank's facilities.'

'In that case,' said the red-haired man, 'let me have me —ing strip lighting back.'

'That's quite impossible, old man,' Garratt said in a tolerant, patient voice which had, even to Balfour, an irritating quality. At times Garratt seemed to listen with satisfaction to his own voice as violinists do to their playing. 'I've already explained that a good deal of this equipment has been installed. And, indeed, is functioning beautifully.'

Balfour walked to the door with the still protesting creditor. 'Don't worry. I'll see my friend settles this. That's a promise. Leave it to me.'

The red-haired man appeared somewhat mollified and went off slowly down the street, turning back once or twice. Suddenly Garratt appeared by Balfour's side and dramatically made a gesture at the retreating figure. It was a gesture which he called 'atropaic', intended to ward off evil spirits, but had a more commonly held, coarse interpretation. Balfour hauled him back into the shop and shut the door.

'You're a nut, Howard. A real absolute twit. Giving him a dud cheque. You could be in serious trouble. You should have asked me.'

Garratt grinned and made the Hindu, prayer-like, sign of welcome. 'You turned up in the – very nick of time.' He capered about the dusty shop in a grotesque dance, apparently swept by a momentary mood of euphoria. Then he sobered up, hunched his back to do a theatrically limping step, and spoke in a very clipped, precise voice:

'What trifling coil do we poor mortals keep;
Wake, eat and drink, evacuate and sleep.'

They went back behind the screens and this time Balfour was able to see that the rear part of the room contained most of Garratt's much-travelled personal belongings. On a shelf there was a gas-ring, a pile of tins and all the other makings for elaborate curries. On the floor a tortoise-shell cabinet, a wicker basket, an enormous tin trunk lettered 'Captain Llewelyn St John Garratt, RN', and two battered cases. The prized sign which had hung outside Garratt's first shop in the Quadrant Arcade leant against a wall. He had made some attempt to bring order among piles of art magazines and reference books, but there were dirty cups and glasses all over the floor and on every other flat surface. There was one canvas-backed chair and an unmade camp bed.

Garratt was absently cleaning his black-and-white shoes, flicking them with a filthy duster. He turned with an expression that showed he now expected some kind of verbal attack, opening his arms wide to show his hopeless position.

'I was absolutely up against it. Got turfed out of Crawford Street *and* lost my rooms. Just had to find a new place and fix it up quick so I could sell some things. I've really slashed prices. Now if I can only get a little luck.' He ended on a note of doubt and morose suspicion.

'I can lend you a hundred. Will that get you straight?' Balfour said shortly.

Garratt made the Hindu prayer-like gesture again and this time Balfour found it rather irritating. 'For which many, many thanks. That should bridge the gap nicely. But I must tell you straight out that Sam lent me fifty when I had to move. Now I suppose I owe it to his estate.'

Balfour stared unbelievingly at Garratt, moved by a quirk of annoyance. 'Honestly – Howard – it's sick-making. To think you were worrying Sam with your unending financial problems when he. . . . When did Sam lend you the money? That was what I really came round to ask you

– when you last saw him and if you knew any reason why he should have done such a thing.'

'Reason why *he* should have done such a thing?' Garratt repeated incredulously. 'Oh, not a chance. Sam? No! You know how he was about heights. Naturally I took it that he'd had an attack by a window, something like that. You don't really think that he could have committed suicide?'

'I don't know,' Balfour admitted. 'But I had a cable from him while I was in Calvi saying that he needed my advice about "a terrible decision". Then the next thing I heard was that he was dead. What was he like when you last saw him? Did he say anything to make you think he was down? Was he ill?'

'I'll have to think. I've seen him quite a lot just recently. You know he often had an evening meal at Smith's the butchers in the Edgware Road. You can get jolly good salt beef sandwiches and lemon tea there. He lent me the fifty quid in Smith's about the middle of last month. I know it was just the time you were going abroad. Then I saw him last – oh, about ten days ago. I wouldn't have said he was depressed but he certainly had something on his mind. He seemed absorbed in a problem, brooding a bit. I remember that evening I came up behind him and noticed he had made a list of names. Well, of course as you know he was always a great one for notes and lists. But this one rather stuck in my head. Quite frankly there was a place-name in it and I thought it might mean that he'd hit on some good little sale that was coming up. As soon as I got back home I looked it up in a Gazetteer, but with no success. I think it was Knowl Green. There's a Knowl Hill in Berkshire but no Knowl Green. Then I thought I might have got it wrong and looked up Bowl Green. No luck with that one either.'

'Knowl Green? Never heard of it,' Balfour said. 'What else was there on the list?'

Garratt hovered in alert speculation for a moment, then picked up a piece of paper and wrote quickly as he tapped on his forehead with his other hand. 'That's it, I think.'

'Knowl Green? Steiner? Quarry?' Balfour studied the list with a frown. 'Doesn't mean a thing to me. But I'll keep it. I've got to see the police about this business – they might be interested.'

'Wait a minute.' Garratt walked up and down with his eyes closed. 'There was another name, I think. Or some word which made me think that Knowl Green *might* be a place where there was a sale. Was it an auctioneer's name? No – well, not one of the big ones anyway. Mmmm. I can't get it. Look, let me make you a curry. This is a fantastic pickle – you should try it. Perhaps the other name will come to me if I do some cooking and empty my mind.' He handed Balfour a jar for inspection, pointing to the label which read 'Fern's BRINJAL pickle, Mrs N. Fernandes, 19 Frere Road, Kirkee, Poona 3'.

'That's the real stuff, bai Jove. Absolutely piping hot. You feel just as if your mouth was on fire!' he added persuasively. Garratt had spent some of his youth in India and was a curry addict who could enjoyably spend an hour choosing ingredients in the Bombay Emporium in Grafton Way. He stolidly persisted in ignoring Balfour's lack of enthusiasm for curries. He set up a card-table and produced a frying-pan from behind a curtain.

'No – thanks all the same.' Balfour took out his chequebook. 'You think about the other name over your lunch. And with this loan I shall expect you to put your affairs in order. Don't forget to pay that red-haired electrician. Then really make an effort to sell some stuff. It shouldn't be that difficult. You've got paintings out there you could take along to Max Weber this afternoon ...'

'I know. But if I knock out all my good paintings in the trade, how am I ever going to build up a private collector's list?'

'Build up ...' Balfour nearly exploded in irritation. 'You ass! What you've got to worry about is not going down the drain! Pay your debts, get straight. *Then* you

71

can think about choosing who you want to sell to. Really!' He waved his hand round at the sleazy set-up. 'Howard, for Christ's sake, pull yourself together! You've got a flair for spotting a good picture but you're about the world's worst businessman. You must sell to dealers, collectors, one-eyed Zulus, anyone who can *pay*!'

Balfour's tirade seemed to have little effect on Garratt, who had weathered many similar storms. He stood with half-closed eyes and a rather smug grin, waving the cheque in order to dry the ink. Then he held his head on one side and moved his fingers up and down as if he was slowly typing out a message. 'Ah. Got it. It was you mentioning dealer. There was another name on that list with Knowl Green, etcetera. L. Spiegl. You know – the inimitable Leo!'

9

'Sorry, but I want to keep the lot intacto as the milkmaid · said to the farmer.'

'He raced through those last few a bit quickish ...'

'He wants his lunch like you and me.'

'Just keep taking the tablets then.'

The book-sale at Sotheby's had ended and the dealers, collectors and a few spectators were dispersing against a background of banter. There was a press of people coming down the narrow steps from the book-room which prevented Balfour ascending, and he waited at the bottom feeling a little frustrated in case Leopold Spiegl slipped out of the St George Street entrance. He had got a taxi direct from Lampeter Parade knowing that Sotheby's was his best chance of contacting Spiegl.

'Balfour.' James Henderson nodded and grimaced – a twitching movement of the pepper-and-salt moustache which bared horse-sized teeth and a good deal of gum. It was a grudging acknowledgement of Balfour's existence which also conveyed the impression that things generally would be better without it. Henderson was one of the 'old school' of dealers who persisted in saying that Balfour was just a lucky speculator, owing his success to his wife's money. They eyed each other levelly. Henderson said gleefully: 'We've seen so little of you recently. I see no point in concealing that we thought you'd had it, professionally-wise.'

Balfour nodded. 'Thank you. Sorry about any disappointment. Have you seen Leo?'

Henderson hesitated a little over the formation of an epigram, giving Balfour a look that made it plain he was not worthy of it: 'Yes. We have been exposed to yet one more example of his traditionally irritating behaviour.'

The question and answer had not been necessary because higher up the stairs Balfour could hear Leopold Spiegl saying 'And you . . . and you,' then laughing hilariously. Henderson gave Balfour's clothes a disgruntled look, examining the dark grey and blue striped blazer, grey button-down shirt, bishop's apron trousers and moccasin loungers with equal disfavour, then moved off.

Spiegl had a world-wide reputation among dealers as being more of a clown or an actor than a businessman – he was said to have attended a summer sale at Christie's in a Hawaiian shirt and Bermudan shorts. But his flamboyance, continual jokes and clowning manner covered an unusual ability to find interesting material and place it without having a permanent address or any proper business premises. From briefly rented rooms or apartments in New York, London, Dublin and Paris he was perpetually 'getting things moving'. Spiegl's vaunted motto was 'I only like to gamble with what I can't afford to lose' and he had handled things as disparate as Farouk's pornography and Robert Browning love-letters.

He appeared round the corner of the stairs, saying tauntingly over his shoulder, 'The name of the game is money. . . . Well, see you in court.' When he saw Balfour he shouted 'Maestro!' and hurried down the last few steps, throwing a flurry of punches in the Rocky Marciano crowding style and ending up by tapping Balfour quite hard on the collar-bone.

Spiegl had a large handsome mobile face, a full head of black curly hair which was going white in an attractive way, and a swarthy complexion. He had missed one or two shaves but still managed to look spruce in a dark brown light-weight suit, pale blue shirt and yellow tie.

'Ned Balfour! A genuine human being!' he exclaimed as if he was introducing him to a television audience. Then he looked round to see if he was in danger of being overheard. 'Do you, or do you not, want in on the biggest deal of the century?'

'I'd like a chat,' Balfour admitted cautiously. 'Have you got time for a coffee?'

'Better yet,' Spiegl said, taking out all the change in a trouser pocket and shifting it round in his hand, 'I have the cash I think to buy you a sandwich in the Grove Street nosh bar.' There was a vaguely continental smell about him, partly compounded of the thin Dutch cigars he smoked and a musky but pleasant soap.

As they made their way past Sotheby's long inquiry counter where people were queuing to pay for their purchases, it was plain that Spiegl was in a febrile mood, calling out to various dealers, 'Put your money where your mouth is,' 'Up yours,' 'Don't give me that old ho-hum.'

When they were in New Bond Street he jubilantly explained to Balfour: 'I swept the board. I spent money that hasn't been minted yet.'

'At least you seem to have annoyed Mr James Henderson,' Balfour said slyly.

'—ing old woman,' Spiegl said. 'All huff and puff. I'd like to put him in a cannon and fire him in the general direction of Constantinople.'

As they turned into Grove Street Spiegl put his hand on Balfour's arm and said confidentially with a disarming grin, 'I got carried away. My bill! I hate to think of it. My bank manager doesn't know that kind of money exists. I might just be prepared to turn some of the loot over at a very small profit.'

Balfour shook his head. 'Sorry, Leo. There wasn't a thing in the sale I needed. I just wanted to see you.'

'Never mind,' Spiegl said. 'I'll still buy you a sandwich. Your credit is good. There's this other deal. So big it's terrifying! In Ireland I'm on the verge of a goldmine!'

Balfour not only knew 'the inimitable Leo' but liked him better than most of the more conventional dealers. Spiegl had the American virtues of generosity, enthusiasm and being outward-going; he had the Jewish ones of quick-wittedness and humour. He did not know that class barriers existed. Balfour had also been exposed to his faults, had suffered in various deals from his unreliability and tendency to bend the truth, but found him, on balance, very congenial. From long experience he knew he would have to wait till Leo's quips and stories were expended before asking him about Sam Weiss and 'Knowl Green', otherwise the question would be brushed aside. 'You can't have the goods if you won't listen to the sales talk' was Spiegl's explanation of his habitual practice in business.

'I'll level with you. In Ireland there's this great archive of manuscripts – literary – just your cup of tea. And I can put the deal through but I must have a library or collector lined up. In other words the owner wants to know where the stuff is going. And the bank roll must be big. I tried to see Mr Leonard Cato – everywhere I hear his name, Cato's bought this, Cato's interested in that – so I make to phone him. The phonemanship at Toller, Cato has to be experienced to be believed! Then I went round there, a miniature skyscraper in the City. Three men fell on me in the hall to undress me and take away my raincoat. One went up with me in the lift to carry my briefcase. Finally I'm in a vast board-room talking to this silver-haired geezer underneath a big clock with a red second hand whizzing round, and there's someone in the corner taking notes. Like I was trying to con the Crown Jewels out of the Tower. I'm really sweating trying to get this deal off the ground. All I wanted for Chrissake was to know whether Mr Leonard Cato was at all interested. Suddenly I discover I'm not even talking to him. It's his "personal assistant". So I'm not big enough to talk to Mr Leonard Cato . . .'

Spiegl broke off to hold up four fingers at the counter: 'Smoked salmon sandwiches. Salmon and butter extra thick. The expense is immaterial. My friend here is a millionaire. One black and one very strong coffee.' He looked gloomily round the room. The effervescence of his Sotheby's mood was gradually being dissipated.

'So I give up on trying to sell this fantastic collection to his bumship Cato. Who the hell does he think he is? You know I heard that Cato isn't even his real name – it's really something like Brown or Smith. He's a phony all through. Then I think of your client. Mrs Phillips isn't it? From what I hear she has all the money there is and her collection has the necessary prestige. What it is – these people in Ireland don't want to sell the stuff to a dealer and think it may be floating round for years yet on the market. But if I can go to them and promise it will disappear without any publicity into the famous Mrs Phillips collection, they'll be ready and willing. How about it, Ned?'

'Could be,' Balfour said thoughtfully. 'I'd want to see a list – she's mainly interested in poetry. But you could use her name to the extent of saying it was a possibility.'

'That's good enough at this stage,' Spiegl said quickly. 'She buys on your say so – I know that. And when you see the haul you'll be keen. And,' he went down on one knee and sang, in a very good imitation of Al Jolson, 'and I'm happy. So-o ha-appy.'

The sandwiches had been brought by a rather pale girl who was obviously impressed by Spiegl's extemporizations – she hovered near by, taking a long time to collect empty cups and plates. Spiegl took a jumbo-sized bite at a sandwich which left only the crust, and winked hugely at the girl. He had an enviable amount of energy, enthusiasm and ambition. In a few minutes he would be out on the street again, 'getting things moving', telling stories, making trans-Atlantic phone calls from other dealers' offices and paying for them in odd mixtures of foreign currencies, shouting, laughing. Balfour always enjoyed listening to him but found it difficult to know what he really felt about life. In particular he had never been able to understand Spiegl's attitude to the Jewish religion – unlike Sammy Weiss Leo paid attention to the observances of the *Shulchan Aruch*, kept strictly to a kosher diet but sometimes seemed to treat the whole business as a joke. Once, in a rare serious mood, he had confided 'Heaven is not in the hereafter'. He said it with great authority, as if the definitive message had just come through. 'There's nothing in the Bible' (by which he meant the Old Testament) 'to make you think otherwise. How are you treating people? Do they like you? Do you love somebody, are you loved in turn? Are you happy? That's your heaven. You make it here.'

Spiegl beckoned to the girl, making eyes at her in a comic fashion, carefully masticating his last sandwich, then said: 'Are you sure this is really Rye bread? Then two more of the same. All on his bill,' indicating Balfour. 'I'm flat broke,' he admitted to the nonplussed girl. 'A human derelict. I couldn't pay for a glass of water. Why, if I break this plate you'll have to sue me.' He turned to Balfour: 'Another Jewish tale for your collection. It's the most sacred day in the Jewish Calendar, *Yom Kippur*, and everyone is in the synagogue beating his breast, atoning for his sins. The beadle sees a woman in the gallery, beating her groin instead. He rushes up to her, crying indignantly, "Don't you know how to atone for your sins?" And the woman as indignantly retorts, "You're telling me where I have sinned?"'

Balfour laughed and Spiegl grinned widely, moving his head vigorously from side to side in time with Balfour's amusement, as if to encourage it. Then he said flatly: 'So O.K. you've been patient. What's your problem?'

'About Sammy Weiss. You heard he was dead?'

'I did. Someone told me. I never knew him well but he seemed a nice little man. He survives Belsen or some such, and then this. That devil Hitler, from his grave he's still killing people. . . . But what about him?'

'Sammy was a great friend of mine,' Balfour explained. 'I knew him about as well as any one person can know another I think. I would have bet all the money there is that he wouldn't kill himself. Yet this happened. I'm mystified. I was abroad at the time but I've been trying to find out if anyone knew what was wrong. The only thing I've come up with is a list he was brooding over. It had your name on it.'

'My name?' Spiegl protested. The joking manner vanished. 'I hardly knew him. Five, six times I've seen him. Exchanged a few polite words. I could have passed him in the street! Why my name?'

'Your name, linked with a place "Knowl Green" and two other names, Steiner and Quarry.'

'I know some Steiners, who doesn't? But "Knowl Green" and "Quarry" I've never heard of ... I don't like it.'

'What do you mean?'

'It's simple. I just don't like the idea – about Mr Weiss and this list. Spiegl – it's not a proprietary brand. There are plenty other Spiegls.'

'It was L. Spiegl on the list.'

'No,' Leo said firmly. 'How can I be involved?' he complained to the room at large. 'What will happen to this list? Have the police got it? It's not fair. The police get hold of this list and the next I know I'm being subpoenaed to attend an inquiry. Something like that. And I know nothing. Just now I can't afford to be waiting around.' He looked down at the calendar on his watch. 'Six days from now I *have* to be in Dublin.' He put his elbows on the table and held his face, waggling it from side to side, repeating 'Weiss? Knowl Green?'

There was a long pregnant silence which emphasized his change of mood. Even the anaemic-looking girl at the counter appeared to have noticed and kept glancing at him as she made piles of sandwiches.

Balfour said, 'Of course it won't make trouble for you. Just a list ...' But Spiegl shook his head to show that such comments were irritating as well as useless. It looked as if some of the air had been deflated from his face, and folds of skin in his neck were more noticeable. His expression was very serious and without his customary ebullience he looked years older. He said, under his breath, 'But it takes two to Tango.' He pulled open his sleek black leather brief case, carelessly spilling a toothbrush, a Ritz Hotel towel and a cream Cossack-style pyjama top on to the table. This kind of emergence always took place when Spiegl was selling something, so Balfour was prepared for any disclosures. From a confusion of toilet things, socks and large manilla envelopes, a gold biro and some business cards were retrieved. The cards were impressively engraved 'Leopold Spiegl & Associates Inc. International Dealers in Manuscripts, Rare Books, Objets d'Art. New York – London – Paris.' Mumbling something in Yiddish he wrote the names Balfour had mentioned on the back of a card,

'Now you've got me worried. Frankly the day is spoilt. From out of the blue this mystery which I don't need. Of course he must have had a reason for writing my name. But I've never heard of "Knowl Green". Does it exist? One hundred per cent sure I've never been there. And there's no connection in the past. Just a few years I've known him – *slightly*. And during the time he was in Belsen or wherever – all through the war years – I never left Crown Heights, Brooklyn.'

10

Balfour walked round Trafalgar Square in a particularly thoughtful mood, feeling rather unreal, like a ghost threading its way through the lively though slow-moving tourists. At his office Miss Bowyer had told him that Detective Superintendent Hanson would like to see him between three and four at the Commissioner's Office, New Scotland Yard. His own feeble detective work now seemed completely pointless – all he had achieved was to upset Spiegl. At first he had been very surprised at that rather emotional disturbance, but on thinking the matter over remembered other occasions when a faintly pusillanimous streak had been suddenly revealed beneath the flamboyance and boasting. There was no doubt in his mind that Leo had been telling the truth in saying that the names on the list meant nothing to him – it seemed likely that what Garratt had seen was just some odd doodling which had nothing to do with Sammy Weiss's brooding.

Balfour was dogged by unformulated apprehensiveness. He was oddly disconcerted as he walked down Whitehall to remember the two pairs of water-skis which he had left at the bottom of the cliff in Corsica. It was a matter of little importance which could be dealt with by a phone call to Roger du Cros, but in his present mood he felt incapable of handling such things. It was the imminent appointment at Scotland Yard that had put him on edge. He was anxious to know any facts that the police might give him, yet there were aspects of the interview which he dreaded. His mind shied away from learning the details – what actually happened to a human body when it was literally smashed against concrete. He had always been squeamish about such things and had to steel himself daily during the war when he had spent months in the skin ward at the Wellhouse Hospital, Barnet, and at East Grinstead, and had seen much worse cases of burns than his own.

As he went past the Cenotaph, knowing he was only minutes away from meeting Hanson, he felt like someone going to receive a long-dreaded verdict on an X-ray; but once he had turned down the short passage-way on his left leading into the Yard the procedure of explaining why he had come, filling in the form with his name and address and following the messenger along the corridor, dispelled his thoughts.

The ground-floor office he entered was a large one looking across the Thames to the London County Council buildings. A lithe man with heavy shoulders and a tanned face greeted him cordially: 'Mr Balfour? My name's Hanson. Take a pew. I've sent for some tea.' The seat he indicated was positioned so that Balfour sat exactly opposite him. Despite the friendly welcome Balfour felt like a schoolboy up before the head-master guiltily searching his mind for any possible crimes. He glanced quickly above Hanson's head at the only visible decoration, a photograph of a beefy rugby team.

The man who faced him was perhaps six or seven years younger than himself, but Balfour was doubtful whether he could handle his side of the interview. In this numb, dull-witted mood questions might have to be put to him twice. Hanson looked very fit and unconcerned, rather like a pro tennis player. He wore a thin grey tweed suit with a white shirt and an unusual tie showing a sword plunged through a golden globe on a maroon silk background. On his desk there were several things ranged in front of him, a small cardboard packet, some pieces of paper, a pocket diary and two books, one of which Balfour recognized as the Concise Oxford Dictionary. It was almost as though a conjuring show had been prepared for his benefit.

Hanson put a blunt fore-finger down on the dictionary and said cheerfully: 'You caught me at my homework. I was just looking up the definition of "vertigo" which I understand Mr Weiss suffered from. ... Should have said of course that it was kind of you to come along. They told me at De Jong's in the Burlington Arcade that you were Mr Weiss's closest friend. And his executor I believe?'

Balfour spoke quickly, as if he was blurting out a confession: 'Yes. But mainly because he wanted me to see that his possessions such as books and pictures should be sold to the best advantage. I don't really know anything about his financial position. You've contacted Holland & Marshall in New Square? They're the solicitors.'

'We have. Only one living relative, we're told, his sister Rebecca Weiss, now living in Tel Aviv?'

Balfour nodded: 'I believe half of anything Sam ... Mr Weiss left will go to her, and half to the "Save the Children" fund.'

Hanson smiled tolerantly as if he didn't mind how much superfluous information he received. He turned the packet round on the desk so that Balfour could read the lettering 'Aventyl'. 'Funny thing but we haven't been able to find out who Mr Weiss's doctor was, but then nobody at De Jong's seems to have known much about his personal life.'

'I'm not surprised,' Balfour explained, 'his only real friend in the firm is the boss in Amsterdam, old Mr Henk De Jong. I know the staff in the Arcade are all much younger men, a different generation. But oddly enough I can't say that I know his doctor either. I don't remember him ever mentioning the name.'

'Well, we must keep digging for that. In these National Health days surely everyone ...? Wasn't he ever ill?'

'Minor things – if you call migraine headaches minor. But not anything really serious that I know about.'

'You see we found this packet near the body. Needn't be his of course. Aventyl. Nortriptyline Hydrochloride, to blind you with science. An antidepressant to relieve anxiety with minimal side effects I'm told. Good stuff, but you have to get it on a prescription from a doctor. I had a word, by the way, with our medico, and he said that vertigo has been explained by some psychologists as the tension between the desire to fall and the dread of falling.' Hanson said this in a tone that suspended belief in the opinions of psychologists. He put his elbows on his desk and steepled his hands, then expelled air in and out of his nostrils noisily inside the little tent so that he sounded as if he was breathing in an iron lung.

Two cups of tea were brought in by a uniformed messenger and Hanson produced some digestive biscuits and then munched one up very quickly. His blue eyes were cold and he had a very calm expression – Balfour could not imagine an event which would surprise or disconcert him much. Suddenly he pushed the tin out of reach as if reminding himself of some regimen of dieting and said: 'Normally D Div. would have handled this. But they're very busy. So they asked me. And then there are one or two things. . . . We've had a postmortem. There will definitely be an inquest. Mr Weiss died from multiple injuries resulting from the fall – broken neck, heart pierced by a fractured rib – either of those could have killed him.' He casually added an afterthought: 'I had a case once in Coventry where a woman fell from about the same height and had much the same injuries. In fact she was mashed up more because she fell over a corrugated iron fence. The body was fully clothed. I ordered a P.M. Found that she'd been stabbed while naked, dressed again with corset, the lot, and then tossed out . . .'

Balfour remained silent, not knowing exactly what his response should be, or even in which direction the conversation was heading.

Hanson turned two of the pieces of paper round so that these too could be read from the other side of the desk. 'We locked up the house and I took a few things away. This cheque, the diary and this typed note. By the way, the house. A house like that in Paley Street off Cheyne Walk, now, surely that would cost a packet?'

'It would today. He thought it was worth perhaps twenty thousand or more but he didn't pay much for it. He snapped it up in '46, badly bomb damaged, at a low figure.'

'I see,' Hanson said reflectively and made a note on a tiny pad. 'He was abroad quite a lot, I take it?'

'Fairly often. Amsterdam every month usually.'

'As much as that?'

'Yes.'

'And this cheque.' Hanson handed it to Balfour who saw that it was from the Overseas Department of Lloyds Bank in Eastcheap, double the size of an ordinary one, with the top half, above a perforated line, bearing information about the sender. 'You see it's dated 25th July, a week before. ... Left lying about on his desk. A thousand pounds – a largish sum – well to me at least.'

Balfour looked at it carefully. The left hand side of the top half bore Sammy's typed name and address and the date – the right hand showed that it had been sent from the Swiss Trade Credit Bank in Zurich by order of External Account Ref. 400990.

'Funny about that cheque,' Hanson said. 'We've been in touch with Mr De Jong and as far as he knows it's got nothing to do with the business. So I tried to take it a step further. Our people contacted the Swiss Trade Credit Bank and came up against the proverbial brick wall. The bank could not divulge the payee. You see, under their federal rule on secrecy, Article 47B, money can be credited to an account known only by a number.' He pulled a wry face. 'Doesn't make our work easier, a thing like that.'

'It's possible that Mr Weiss sold something in Zurich,' Balfour volunteered. 'He collected pictures, curios, and he did get some valuable things. Never spent a great deal but he had a wonderful eye ...'

Hanson cleared his throat as though he was not impressed with this. 'No other ideas, suggestions? Any reason why he should keep the cheque and not bank it? Was he usually punctual, business-like?'

'Oh yes. Meticulous. Hated to owe anyone a penny. Every bill was paid the day it came in. Rather an obsession with him.'

'So, you see. That's exactly what I heard from Mr De Jong. It's not in character. Puzzling. . . . Then this diary. Naturally I've been through it closely. Shows an interesting mind – sensitive I thought. But you'll see there are no entries after the 18th July and a gap of more than two days is otherwise rare. And there's one older entry I thought I should mention. Now where is it? 24th March, I think. Yes, this.'

Balfour looked at the diary and read in Weiss's even, sharply sloping hand:

> The Rose is red. ye Gras
> is green : the Days are past
> Which I have seen All ye yt
> on me Cast & Eye : as you are
> now So once was I but as I
> am now So shall ye be Pre
> pare for Death and follow
> me

Balfour shook his head decisively. 'No. For once I can be helpful in a negative way. That has no significance. Just an old epitaph. He had been collecting them for years, was compiling an anthology of unusual ones. I've often written one down for him on my travels.'

'A rather morbid interest, isn't it?'

'Not really. He looked on it purely as a form of art. They can be quite fascinating.'

'Right,' Hanson said. 'That is useful. You see – together with the Aventyl tablets it rather had me going for a while.' Balfour got the impression that it had been in a direction which Hanson had already abandoned before this interview: he would have liked to ask pointblank what Hanson's present theory was but knew it would be useless.

86

'This typed note,' Hanson went on, holding up a quarto sheet with some lines eccentrically typed at the top, 'I found in the diary, folded up and inserted at the last entry.'

The page contained instructions:

Go to the office of the Registrar of Companies in City Road. Pay your shilling and get handed a form.

Look up the firm you want to study in the index. It appears under the first letter of its first name (thus Bertram Kittredge Ltd would be under 'B').

Write the number on your form and hand it in. In exchange you will be given a numbered disc. The number corresponds to a desk, at which, in five minutes or so, the file of the relevant company will be deposited. What the file contains will depend on the nature of the company. Articles of Association will be there. Names, addresses and occupation of directors are given.

'It looks,' Hanson said, 'as if he might be checking up on some company. He hadn't mentioned to you any dodgy investment, buying shares? Anything like that?'

'Never. As far as I know he didn't own a share.'

'O.K.' Hanson made another note. 'And the place where it happened, this Bowdon Court. Naturally the first thing Sergeant Lowther did, he asked round to see if anyone living there knew Mr Weiss, but he drew a blank. You can't help about that?'

'I'm afraid not. I didn't know it existed.'

'Oh, quite a largish block of flats. Fronts on to Norfolk Square which is busy enough. But the side where it happened is in a cul-de-sac.'

'I – wanted to ask you if you thought there was any chance of it being an accident?'

Hanson gave Balfour a brief sympathetic look. With a finger tip he thoughtfully traced an unapparent line in his forehead. 'Shouldn't think so. Because of the window – "They were never opened" the porter said, but how do we know it wasn't open this time? – it's *just* possible. But it's stretching coincidence a bit. A man with vertigo climbs ten floors and then has an attack in front of a window that by some freak chance is open. Then again from the position of the body it looks as if he had moved along a ledge beneath the window before he fell.'

'I see.'

'Well, many thanks for all your help.'

Balfour thought he was being dismissed and began to move in his chair, but Hanson said, 'I must keep you a minute more. They won't let you out of here till I've signed that form they gave you.'

Balfour looked in his pocket, finding it scrawled up with another piece of paper. 'God!' he exclaimed, 'I nearly forgot, you'll think I'm an idiot. I brought this along to show you. It's the cable I received in Corsica from Weiss before I had another one from my wife to say that he was dead.'

Hanson threw him an unmasked look in which there was a mixture of surprise, irritation and contempt. He seemed to hover on the edge of an exclamation but when he spoke it was in a slow, slightly sarcastic voice: 'Thank you. I should like to see it.'

He examined the cable form intently, then said: 'Well, I'm glad you remembered this. Better late than never. No, that's not fair. Bit of luck you kept it. You won't mind if I hang on to it for the time being?'

Balfour woke with a gasp and a movement of revulsion away from a vision of a falling body hitting the ground with a jarring, sickening thud. He had consciously made an effort to avoid thinking of this subject but his unconscious had represented it to him, like a horrid meal that had to be eaten up. Sir Thomas Browne had written, 'We are more than ourselves in sleep, and the slumber of the Body seems to be but the waking of the Soul', and Balfour had often found that dreams served him up with a slightly altered version of a day-time problem. He knew he had no reason for feeling guilty about Weiss's death, but all the same it seemed certain he would not be released from this unease until he at least understood why it happened.

As he began to shave he was struck by an idea and, face half-covered in lather, he phoned Inquiries to see if there was a telephone exchange called 'Knowl Green' but without success. He had already checked Garratt's assertion that the place was not listed in a gazetteer. Continuing his shave, he realized that the image of the falling body was not of Weiss but had come back to him from a film he had seen years before about the Eiffel Tower. One of the incidents shown in the history of the tower was the attempt of a man to fly in the early 1900's with large bird-like wings made of canes and feathers attached to his arms. There had been some badly lit preliminary shots, spotted with 'rain', showing his friends moving about jerkily, making preparations, pointing dramatically, giving him encouragement and advice. Then there was a touching close-up of the poor devil, hovering alone by the parapet, fear apparent in his staring eyes, unable for some moments to summon up courage for the take-off. A blurred image followed – the horrifying instant when he leapt, pathetically moving his cumbersome wings before they twisted round him like a shroud. Then a shot taken from the ground, showing him plummeting down like an ungainly giant moth. Finally the early moving camera, to the mildly ironical commentary by Alexander Woollcott, inspected the foot-deep dent in the tarmac made by the 'bird-man'.

As Balfour made *muesli* and coffee, fragments from his talk with Superintendent Hanson returned to him against his will. After leaving Scotland Yard he had returned to Jermyn Street and dictated business letters, doing a good deal of routine work before setting out on a deliberate programme of swimming and playing squash to leave himself so tired that he could get to sleep without thinking about the interview. But now the inexplicable matters of the unpaid £1,000 cheque, the typed note about research on Companies at the City Road registry, recurred uselessly. He wondered about the significance of Hanson's questions about Sam's trips abroad. In a way his contribution to the police inquiries had been inadequate, but anything else he could have volunteered would have been based purely on his own opinions and therefore of debatable value. He could have assured Hanson, on that basis alone, that there was no possibility of Sam being mixed up in smuggling or anything else illegal, but what value could Hanson put on such a statement?

When he reached his office Balfour felt more inclined to settle to his own work. He accepted now that his friends did not know of any cause for the death, and if anyone was going to unravel the mystery it would have to be the police. Hanson seemed a dogged and very capable person to conduct the inquiry.

Jane Lupton was busy with the addressograph files, working on the list of changes of address. She said, 'Miss Bowyer's at the British Museum. Doing some research on that imperfect fourteenth-century manuscript. Said it was no more difficult than the Synoptic problem.'

'Oh yes,' Balfour moved off into his own room and shut the door. He knew very little about early manuscripts and nothing about the problem of the Synoptic Gospels, but he liked to keep this position fairly vague as far as Miss Lupton was concerned. It was understood that early material was Miss Bowyer's province, but there was no point in underlining his own ignorance of the subject. The fact that Patricia Bowyer was so efficient and practically capable of running the business by herself was one of the reasons for his losing interest in it to some degree. Another important factor was the comparative ease with which they now made money. They had some good and a few excellent customers – they seemed to attract more without advertising and had no difficulty in finding enough material; it was all a little too easy now. Despite what people like James Henderson said, he had never used his wife's money and in the early years it had been a struggle – he had enjoyed it then.

Balfour adjusted the mechanical calendar on his desk to 4/8/66. In two days he would be forty-three. A typical Leo, vain and conceited – 'The man who always reaches for the bill in a restaurant.' He had reached middle age, the period of sensing one's limitations and rapidly dwindling perspectives, without achieving much.

He opened the *Daily Telegraph* and read an account of the previous day's sale at Christie's, noting that Max Weber Ltd had acquired paintings by Carel Fabritius, Nicolaes Muys and Hendrik Rietschoof. His own success was nothing when compared with Max's, but Max's ambition knew no limits whereas his own was practically non-existent. He had no idea what he really wanted from life.

Jane Lupton knocked and put her head round the door. 'Sorry but I forgot a phone message. From Mr Garratt. Said to tell you it might be Knoll Green. A green knoll struck a chord. O.K.?' She made a shrugging gesture to imply that she took no responsibility for the sanity of Garratt's suggestions.

'Yes. Thanks. That's O.K., I know what he means. Oh, by the way, make an address plate for Leonard Cato Esq. Ennismore Gardens, Kensington, I think. But if he's not listed in the phone-book simply send it to Toller, Cato, in the City somewhere.'

Balfour did not bother to write down Garratt's revised text. He had remembered that he must phone Miss Phelips. He could indulge in as much self-congratulation as he liked about the thriving state of his business, but if he lost Miss Phelips' custom the position would be rather different. And of course it pleased a Leo to be able to walk into Sotheby's or Parke-Bernet when an important poetical manuscript was being sold knowing that he could come decisively into the bidding at a late stage – in that at least he resembled Max.

The Roehampton number was answered by Miss Leighton who was Miss Phelips' secretary and companion. She worked part-time on the manuscript collection and was genuinely keen about it, often commenting about things 'being saved from going to the States'. She sounded as cheerful and friendly as usual and went off humming. Balfour heard her clicking retreating steps on the parquet floor and a snatch of *All I want is a room somewhere*.

But as soon as Olivia Phelips came on the phone he knew something was wrong. She asked him if he could come to see her right away and he agreed to go that afternoon. She said, 'Between four and five?' instead of her usual suggestion that he should stay for tea. Her tone was definitely cool. There was no inquiry about his holiday, no comment on the fact that he had returned before the day Miss Bowyer had mentioned. To his ear, usually fairly sensitive to people's reactions, there was the subtle suggestion of a reproach in her tone. He replaced the phone after a brief leave-taking and said quietly, 'Yikes.'

He was baffled by this situation. If Olivia Malise Phelips was his idea of the perfect customer, it was equally plain the firm of T. Edward Balfour respected that and made every effort to keep her happy. What could they possibly have done to annoy her? She must realize the care with which they handled her requests. Then apart from the business side of their relationship there was, he had thought, a genuine friendship. He found her sympathetic and attractive and had always imagined that she was reasonably fond of him. It was true they had argued about a number of things. She was more politically inclined than he was, and contributed funds to the Liberal Party; a devout Quaker where he was an agnostic. She was a pacifist while he thought some things were worth fighting for. But these were differences between friends who respected each other's point of view. And for people with such widely differing backgrounds – his childhood had been a middle-class London suburban one in the 20s and 30s, whereas hers was Victorian and Edwardian in the patrician atmosphere of Crabbe's Park's Jacobean brick, crow-stepped gables and coffered ceilings – they had many interests in common.

Balfour thought back to the last time he had driven Olivia to Malmesbury. She took a coquettish delight in the speed with which they crossed the Cotswolds. 'This really is a rather splendid, dashing car,' she had said about his Lancia. It had been a glorious June day when they had walked first amongst the ruins of the house, still smelling of mildew, soot and damp plaster, and then in the parkland with its great summer trees, the towering oaks and elms haunted by birds. Silently they had made their way beyond the trees to a stream where they had seen yellow wagtails and the occasional exciting blue flash of the kingfisher.

On the south side of the ruined house there was a small ornamental lake, edged at one side with a weathered brick wall and the ramshackle remains of a disintegrating boathouse. She looked about her with a sad expression and Balfour could sense how redolent of memories this former pleasure-ground must be – the laughter and voices which would still echo for her about the lily-covered water now frequented only by fat carp and golden orphe and green whirring dragon-flies. Finally they had picnicked on a hill overlooking the house, on a thin skin of turf as much thyme as grass, with a sky resonant with larks. From that vantage point the ruins were even more impressive. The house of honey-coloured stone had been largely destroyed by fire in 1946, and years of disuse since then had seen further roof-fallings so that its only possible future was demolition. For the time being it was a memorial to the evanescence of human hopes and endeavours. The generations of the proud Phelips family, Jacobeans, Georgians, Edwardians, what had they been but insubstantial shadows silhouetted against the background of eternity, so soon to be engulfed forever? It was plain that Olivia Phelips felt this too. She had smiled wryly and quoted Tennyson, 'The woods decay, the woods decay and fall ...'

'Can I speak to Mr Balfour?' In his pleasant day-dream about Crabbe's Park the phone must have rung and he had picked it up without being aware of doing so.

'Yes. This is Balfour.'

'Mr *T. E.* Balfour?'

Balfour's second affirmation was rather impatient.

'All right old lad, I had to check.' The voice at the other end was slow and noticeably short-breathed, perhaps asthmatic. Balfour asked who was speaking.

'Never mind about that. Have you seen Steiner?'

It was a name well calculated to excite Balfour's interest. Various ideas raced through his head. So Garratt had been right about the name Steiner at least. He found it difficult to decide what to say and tried 'No. Why? Should I have seen him?'

There was no comment on this and for a moment he feared that the man had rung off. But listening intently he picked up a very faint consultation going, an exchange between the breathy voice and a quiet one that chattered like a monkey. He could make no sense of what they said.

Then there was a sound as if a bellows was being pumped and the laboured breathing and slow talking began again. 'Right, then. Do you want to hear about Steiner?' Balfour agreed to this without thinking it through, mainly to keep the conversation going. He began to formulate questions but dropped them when the anonymous voice asked him how long it would take him 'to get to Felton Road, leading into Edgware Road, near Marble Arch'.

Balfour glanced at his watch. It was 10.40. 'I can make it by eleven.'

'O.K. then. 12B Felton Road it is. We'll have a little chat.'

Before Balfour could say anything else the line went dead. He dropped the phone, went through Jane Lupton's room without saying anything, and had run along to Lower Regent Street within a minute.

12

'THE CALEY PROPERTY CO.' was the type-written name on the grubby card thumb-tacked by the bell to No. 12B Felton Road. It was at the side of a seedy looking Indian restaurant. There was no response when Balfour rang the bell, so after a minute he walked up the uncarpeted splintering wooden stairs. The cream plaster walls he passed were bare apart from some pencilled *graffiti*. The Caley Company's sign was stencilled in black on a shabby, pale green door which hung open. He knocked and then walked into an empty room. There was not a single piece of furniture in the place and only a small mirror and a calendar decorated with a nude girl on the wall. The green lino-covered floor was filthy, littered with cigarette ends, used matches and odd scraps of paper. He went to the window and looked out into the empty street. A phone began to ring and he realized it was coming from behind another door which he had taken to be a cupboard. He opened it and found another, very small room, again bare apart from a large carton and a phone on the floor. He picked up the phone tentatively, holding it a little way from his ear as if it might explode, noticing that the wall facing him bore a number of phone numbers and had a pattern of small holes where it had been used for darts. The carton contained a large number of empty bottles. The room stank of beer and stale cigarette smoke.

'Balfour! You made it quick! We saw you go in.' The asthmatic voice ended the sentence on an accusing note.

'I came here as you said. Is this some kind of joke?' Balfour felt tense and his chest was tight – he was having a little trouble in breathing himself.

'No, Skipper. Just a little obstacle course to see if you are really keen about Steiner. Now you can meet me pronto, just round the corner. 14 Hyde Park Place. No more tricks. Wait where you are for five minutes. Bert Caley won't mind you loitering on his property – I promise you that.' There was a kind of choky laugh.

Balfour was willing to complete the obstacle course in order to hear about Steiner. He went into the larger office and opened the window to get some fresh air. In the mirror he glimpsed his face, white and strained and the nostrils pinched. At least it made a change from the 'selfish expression'.

He looked at the calendar. The top-heavy, sultry nude was the one chosen for July, so it looked as if the office had only recently been vacated. The tenant had been a careful man in one respect, for all the previous months of the calendar had been carefully turned over rather than torn off. With his toe he moved round a small piece of paper on which there was a list of small sums totalled and boldly ticked.

He waited five minutes and then left the Caley Property Co. feeling prepared for more or less anything. Nevertheless 14 Hyde Park Place managed to surprise him. It was a large church-like building set well back from the road which he must have passed hundreds of times when going up and down the Bayswater Road. There were high iron railings and these helped to obscure it from the road.

He opened the gate and walked nearly up to the building before he realized that it had a deserted air. It was the odd kind of place that had a fascination for him, and he wondered about its history. There was some lettering about welcoming footsore weary travellers over one of the doors. It was only when he was really close that he saw there was only the shell of the building.

He looked cautiously through one of the doors, seeing roofless walls and the sky. He smelt fish oil before he sensed danger. Then he was yanked through the open space and swung round, his arms being expertly pinioned against a wall by two bored-looking youths in dark mohair suits with modish short haircuts like professional football players.

It was a big, fat, totally bald man who smelt of fish-oil. 'Christ,' he said explosively, 'you are a —ing nosey one! I've met some cases. I suppose if we'd told you to put your head ...' He had run out of breath and did not bother to finish the sentence. He spoke with continuously bared teeth and held his face very close to Balfour's, watching him with a fixed expression of mild perplexity. He gave a short laugh and his heavy face moved in sections. 'I think he must be a bit dolly dimple,' he explained to one of the youths.

Balfour noticed that there was a fourth man in dark glasses holding a brindled boxer on a very short steel chain. He had a pale face and an unusually thick mop of black wavy hair rising steeply from a widow's peak. He wore a beige gaberdine suit with a thin black roll-neck pullover and a black leather belt with a large circular silver clasp. He looked like a homosexual of the rare, vicious kind.

The big bald man put his face even closer to Balfour's, staring right into his eyes as if he wanted to hypnotize him. 'Now let me mark your card for you. You're too —ing nosey for your own good.' He moved back a pace and slapped Balfour's face twice in quick succession. They were practised blows delivered in an expert manner with the hand held limp and used like a whip. Balfour could taste the Bovril flavour of blood and a little moisture obscured his eyes.

The bald man did his choky short-breathed laugh again and appealed to one of the youths, 'Stop me. I'm beginning to enjoy it.'

The youth sniggered a little but more as if it was required of him than a genuine response. Even though his face was hot with pain Balfour was struck by the complete indifference of both youths who held his arms. It was quite plainly just a job as far as they were concerned – they were not involved apart from doing the simple labouring work.

'You haven't said anything yet,' the big man said. He had come close again and the fish-oil smell was very strong. He seemed a little impressed by Balfour's silence. Balfour said, 'Are you Steiner? You're standing on my foot.'

'Ah, lippy and still —ing nosey,' the big man said with satisfaction. 'I like that. No – see – I'm – not Steiner.' The sentence was punctuated with pauses as he took hold of Balfour's ears and folded them up in various ways. It was an exercise that had never occurred to Balfour before, but the big man knew how to do it so that it was very painful. The movements disclosed hairy wrists, both of which were tattooed, one with a dolphin and anchor, the other with the words 'H.M.S. Hell-raiser'. He stepped back and slapped once more, a swingeing blow which made Balfour's cheek feel as if it had been set on fire. The big man watched his reaction with considerable interest, as if he was conducting a scientific experiment.

'The form is,' he explained, 'you get pressure until you start minding your own —ing business and forget all about Weiss and Steiner. Get it into your nut once and for all that you can't do any good nosing around. Your old pal Sammy Weiss was bent. When the heat was on he couldn't take it.' He stopped to pump up breath a bit to continue. 'What you *can* do is stir up a bit of trouble for us and that will mean plenty of stick for you. What I mean, if you have any long-term plans, like walking round next week without crutches, you do what I say. Right, Don?'

'Don', the thin youngish man dressed in beige gaber-dine. approached with the fierce-looking dog. 'Don' had high cramped shoulders and a narrow chest. He took off his dark glasses to reveal sea-green eyes which were un-naturally bright, and gave Balfour a merciless, appraising look which was more frightening than anything the big man had done. When he opened his feverish eyes it was as if a microscope had been fractionally adjusted. He moved with the awkward, unreliable gait of someone with an incipient disease of the spine. It was plain that giving Balfour 'plenty of stick' might divert him for a while. He said nothing but nodded and smiled faintly.

'Right. So have we got it straight *now*?' the big man asked patiently. 'If you still want to nose in it can only mean trouble all round. Did you know that your yid friend had been taking really big money? If you stir things up it will mean that his old sister won't get the loot. Her Majesty's —ing Government will grab the lot.' The fact that these men knew of Rebecca Weiss, together with the £1,000 cheque, forced Balfour to consider the possibility that Sammy had been mixed up in something shady. How else could they have known Sammy well enough to be aware that he had a sister who had lived in Tel Aviv for the past eight years?

'O.K.?' the big man inquired. 'Now this is the drill. First they,' he motioned to his silent assistants, 'they let your arms drop. You're stupid you lash out at me. I clobber you or Don sets the dog on you. *You're smart* we all just walk away. You wait here five minutes. You've learnt your lesson all right. If you're upset, well just lay down here and kick and scream a bit. No one will mind. It's very private.' He paused significantly, then added: 'We could have buried you here but you're being given a chance.'

His two assistants stepped back at some unseen signal and Balfour's numb arms dropped limply to his side. He made no movement and 'Don', the boxer dog and the two youths walked off through the doorway.

The chief inquisitor seemed a little reluctant to leave the scene of his recent triumph. He still watched Balfour closely as if he found it hard to believe that things had worked out so nicely. He tapped his forehead and conceded, 'You're sharp. I thought so when I first saw you.

You're quick enough to learn. Now, five minutes remember. You've no reason, play your cards right, ever to see us again.' He lurched out of sight saying: 'Well cheerio Skipper. All right?'

13

From a good viewpoint, half-way across London Bridge, Balfour idly watched the activity by the Custom House and the numerous wharves and jetties between Morgan's Lane Stairs and Tower Bridge. His mind was trying to deal with the puzzle of why Sammy Weiss should have been in contact with the fat bald man. He had to concede that it was just possible that Sammy had been involved in some kind of criminal activity. Supposing he had, and that the offence was smuggling – Superintendent Hanson had underlined the frequency of Sammy's trips to Amsterdam – then this could well have been the reason for the telegram, VITAL I HAVE YOUR ADVICE ON TERRIBLE DECISION I MUST MAKE. ... Perhaps the decision had been to do with Sammy clearing out of England, or about the other men involved, the mysterious Steiner and Quarry? In that event it became possible that the big fat man and his gang worked for Steiner, and had been sent to make sure that no one followed up any leads linking Sammy to Steiner. But in that case how would they know that he might have got on to Steiner's name? It was true that Sammy was always making notes. Or did the gang know of the cable that he had been sent without being sure of its contents?

Balfour gingerly felt his sore nose. One thing was certain – if Sammy killed himself because he was mixed up in crime of some kind, then he did not intend to do any more inquiring or even pass on Steiner's name to Hanson. He was not interested in retrieving money for 'Her Majesty's —ing Customs' at the expense of another interview with 'Don' and the others. He would be content to let Detective Superintendent Hanson make any discoveries in that area. Fortunately there was one person who might be able to tell him about the bald man's gang. 'Chas.' Squibb boasted that he knew most things that went on in London, and from his stories it sometimes seemed that this was true. The Lamb Tavern at lunchtime was the place to find 'Chas.'

The little cut in the underside of Balfour's lip had dried up within minutes of the blow that had caused it; his face still felt flushed but that was probably due to excitement and nervous tension more than the expert slapping – he had suffered much more punishment from so-called 'friendly' boxing matches. The few minutes behind No. 14 Hyde Park place had left no scars and had probably led him to the end of his useless quest. It was a fine warm day and he was looking forward to a peaceful afternoon at Roehampton.

He glanced once more across the river and noticed with surprise that one of the largest warehouses was boldly lettered 'Toller, Cato – Export, Import'. The Southwark side of the Thames was an area he had explored and knew reasonably well, from Clink Street to Tooley Street, the George, the Anchor Inn and the Globe Theatre. He had been over there more than a dozen times and yet he could not remember seeing the Toller, Cato sign before. Perhaps he had but it only impinged now because he had begun to take an interest in the possibility of making Mr Leonard Cato a customer.

Balfour entered Leadenhall Market from its main entrance in Gracechurch Street. He liked many of the London markets, particularly the lesser-known ones in Hessel Street and Douglas Way, but Leadenhall was his favourite. Nearly everything about it appealed to him, the Victorian atmosphere, the elaborate cast-iron work with griffons supporting the City's coat of arms, the brightly lit butchers' shops looking like Dutch still-life paintings, and above all the Lamb Tavern.

At 1 p.m. Balfour was standing at a comparatively quiet

end of the bar, holding a delicious York ham sandwich with plenty of mustard and a half-pint of best bitter. He was savouring the cockney talk going on round him, and mentally contrasting the atmosphere with that of the Malise house where he would be in a few hours' time.

'I've been looking *everywhere* for you.' It was a falsely petulant voice, a ridiculous imitation of a pansy's recrimination. Balfour turned round to see 'Chas.' Squibb shaking the stump of a forefinger at him. He seemed to be even more bald than the last time Balfour had seen him – the thin strands that barely connected his grizzled sideburns with the fringe at the back of his head had suffered further depletion. Squibb was an inch or two shorter than Balfour but had impressively wide shoulders and a barrel chest. He looked extremely prosperous in a dark blue suit, immaculate white shirt and a military striped tie. There was a cornflower in his buttonhole. His shoes shone with a very high polish.

Squibb reached towards the bar and, unsummoned, a pint tankard of Guinness was put into his hand. His red face glistened as though it too had been well polished, and his bright eyes went quickly round the bar, anxious not to miss anything. 'I'll drink to that, by God!' he said, à propos of some overheard remark. Then, to Balfour, 'You know that buy you put me on to? Leominster? The poor old cow with rheumatism? I liked her. And there were some good things there. All those paper-weights. Some Bristol glass tear-bottles and a few other useful odds and sods.' With his free hand, from which two fingers were missing, he took hold of Balfour's lapel. 'Where you been mate, doing a stretch?'

Before Balfour said anything, he added a complaint: 'This morning I went out nearly as far. They said it was like Buck House but it was a right load of old schmutter! You see, everyone's an antique dealer today. So they say! Young know-nothing kids. Still, after all, they just act as clearing-houses for pros like you and me. Well, where have you been hiding yourself?'

'I've been abroad. A holiday in Corsica. So you followed up the tip about Leominster? Did you do all right with the stuff?'

Before speaking further, Squibb took out an extremely thick pile of five pound notes held together by a yellow elastic band, peeled off four and stuffed them down in Balfour's top pocket. 'There you are, boy. I spent seven five oh with the old dear. No chicanery mind, I could have got the stuff for five oh oh. But I still made a profit. So there's a few nicker on account.'

Balfour raised his eyebrows.

'On account of I'm not giving you any more –' Squibb went into a fit of laughing which ended in his belching and saying, 'File that under miscellaneous.'

Balfour wondered about Squibb's attitude to doing favours and how he would respond to a request for information. Squibb was a funny mixture – he was resolutely opposed to anything he considered sentimental, 'Don't give me none of that Sally Army stuff,' but he always seemed friendly enough. Although Balfour had been frank about his 'five week war' Squibb had, for purposes of reminiscence, enrolled him in the 8th Army and sometimes took him conversationally through battles along the North African coast, the Sicily landing at Pachino, and then up the Adriatic to the Pescara River where he had lost two fingers. 'You remember that day,' he would say, ignoring Balfour's protests, 'when we wus at Fuggia,' or some other Italian town atrociously mispronounced, 'and Nobby Clark ...'

'I wanted to ask you a small favour,' Balfour said. 'Just a question.'

'And the prize,' Squibb joked, 'will be, don't tell me, a chocolate smoking set.' But he looked a trifle anxious. He did not care much for a serious conversation and steered away from it, preferring life to be a simple round of work, nosh-ups, knees-ups and bunk-ups. He lacked all curiosity about what made other people tick. 'All right, go on then – this question.'

'I had some trouble this morning,' Balfour said quickly, then pulled his lip slightly outwards to show where it was cut. 'But I didn't get into a fight. I was knocked about by a big chap who seemed used to doing it. About fourteen stone. Six foot two. Tattooed wrists, one with the words "H.M.S. Hell-raiser". He had three other men with him. And a boxer dog.'

Squibb gave Balfour a funny, vacant look – it was as if a plug had been disconnected somewhere so that the light in his eyes had been extinguished. He was silent for once, fingering a badly sewn scar that ran down the side of his forehead.

'You know him,' Balfour said excitedly, 'I can see you know him.'

'You don't do a bad job on description,' Squibb admitted grudgingly. Then he asked: 'What you been up to, mate?'

'Me!' Balfour expostulated. 'Me – *I've* done nothing! It was him. I just stood there and he slapped me around.'

'No, you don't understand, matey. This man, the big chap. *If* I've got him right, he doesn't go round picking on people. It's strictly business with him. Take it from me, you've stepped out of line somehow . . .'

'No – I'll tell you what happened – a friend of mine died, killed himself, I think. And I've been going around, asking a few questions. That's all. I've never seen or heard of this big chap before.'

'I see.' Squibb took a big gulp which emptied his tankard of Guinness and relapsed into silence, continuing the impressive pause by rolling his eyes in silent askance. Then he opened a packet of crisps and, tilting his head back, poured the contents into his mouth without regard for the whereabouts of the little blue packet of salt. 'Well – what you want to know – his name?'

'Yes, his name. . . . But what I really wanted to find out was the kind of racket he was in. Why he should have been tied up with my friend.'

'You don't want much, I'll say that for you.' Squibb

breathed in deeply, holding his nostrils deflated while he thought this over. 'Look, I'll take a chance but do yourself a favour and don't go "asking a few questions" about him.' He looked about him and inquired quietly, 'He's got a nice head of skin like me?'

Balfour nodded.

'It sounds very like Victor Maddox. I've sometimes seen him in the Glib Club in Dean Street.'

'Does he own this place, the Glib Club?'

'No, he doesn't own anything apart from a smart-looking blonde bird, and a big baby-blue American car. He has a kind of debt-collecting agency. Well, that's his usual work. Look, you're a half-wide mug collecting rents and you decide it would be nice not to hand the loot over to the landlord, or you lose a packet at blackjack and give a club a kite, then Mr Victor Maddox calls round and you pay up quick.'

Squibb looked straight at Balfour, saying, 'Now you know me, I'm no jam-puff,' and waited for Balfour to nod agreement. 'But I wouldn't want a call from old Vic. He's a bit short of breath and getting a fat gut but don't let that fool you. He's a really hard case – done two stretches for GBH. And he's always got some real young tearaways in tow. If you put the police on to him he'd just call round again later and you would really find out what "grievous bodily harm" means.' Squibb looked quite concerned.

Balfour said, 'No. It's all right. I think that my curiosity has been satisfied. I hope I shall manage to keep clear of Mr Victor Maddox and the Glib Club.'

Squibb rubbed his hands together. 'That's more like it.' He wheeled round to the bar and tapped himself on the chest, signifying that he wanted another Guinness. 'And a double Cutty Sark here for my friend. You come round again one evening,' he said to Balfour, 'and we'll have another knees-up. My girl Doreen, she likes those old songs you know.' He looked faintly surprised. 'You know a few even I don't. That one "You can see a lot of things at the seaside", and what's that one "You could see as far as Wimbley if it wasn't for the houses in between". And you do the best Harry Champion imitation I know. No boy, we can't afford to lose you.'

14

Woodsmoke was the ambience of the Malise Estate. There was a rambling area of rhododendron and laurel bushes that formed a nearly impenetrable barrier round it and Olivia Malise Phelips' gardeners fought a running battle with the laurel, appearing to be perpetually engaged in making bonfires. The smell of wood burning was one that Balfour particularly liked – more than anything else it evoked the atmosphere of autumn for him, and so it often seemed to be that peaceful, enjoyably melancholy season once he had passed the heavy iron gates and white stone piers surmounted by an eighteenth-century stone-mason's conception of rampant lions. He looked round at a spider's web outlined by the sun and saw a missel-thrush fastidiously hunting for grubs on the gravel drive, flicking over the large laurel leaves with its beak. The London streets were like an alien, neurotic world.

There was a trace of the honey-like perfume of buddleia in the air, and the damp smell of leaf-mould as well as woodsmoke, but Balfour could tell that on this occasion apple branches were being burnt. Olivia had a passion for birds and trees, which was not shared by her gardeners. One of the old men had explained the position to Balfour – how all the trees 'with their great roots, some as thick as your thigh, are ruining the garden, but Miss Phelips she won't see it.'

The Malise estate was of considerable size and was still marked in capital letters on large scale maps, though Olivia had given nearly half of it away when she had built a school. The gardeners could remember when the gardens had been 'double the size, fully staffed and kept up proper'. On the other hand Balfour could foresee the time, not far off, when the garden might not be kept up at all. He was feeling obsessed with a sense of change. After traversing a large section of London in the morning he had spent the early part of the afternoon slowly walking round Richmond and Petersham, where he had lived for a year as a child. With buildings springing up everywhere and the complicated preparations for new roads, the whole of London and its suburbs seemed to be writhing like a gigantic ugly chrysalis, threatening to break out into a new concept of life in which large private estates would have no part. If it had a future, if it was not to be torn down fulfilling some planner's dream of the future, then Olivia's house, with a much reduced stretch of garden, would probably become the headquarters for some business organization. The prospect for the ilex tree, the ancient mulberries and the great pink magnolia was uncertain at best. Soon the thin lawn, in which *parterres* of flowers now glittered in the sun like metallic objects, might be the site for a municipal building or support a motor-way. Balfour had no vested interest in great estates and was not a reactionary regarding many changes, but he did not like to think of those that would take place where he was walking.

Brooding on these things, he was half-way up the horseshoe steps that led to the old house before he remembered that this visit was unlikely to be as pleasant as former occasions. He looked at the cut and moulded bricks which appeared an apricot colour in the sun. It was a Commonwealth house constructed in 1650 by some unknown artisan builder to the order of William Malise, a merchant who had supported Cromwell. The Netherlands influence was apparent in the simple but pleasing design, striking in its regularity, the absence of gables and the handling of the brick-work with bold cornices running across the façade like those on the Dutch house at Kew. The front door was open, and Balfour walked into the hall darkened by the massive oak staircase which had military trophies in the pierced balustrades and carved figures of 'New Model Army' soldiers on the newel posts.

His approach had apparently been noticed upstairs as Patricia Leighton came down half-way and called: 'Olivia won't be long. She's been gardening. Would you care to go in there? I know you can amuse yourself.'

The room she indicated was a large one with very high french windows along one side overlooking the biggest lawn, and it contained a number of things which Balfour liked to look at. It was sparsely furnished but the carpet was a spinach-green Gobelin and there were Cromwellian chairs and a seaweed marquetry desk. The Phelips and Malise families before Olivia had not been collectors but the house contained their random acquisitions over four centuries, including things salvaged from Crabbe's Park. On a Regency card-table there was a 'Doctor Wall' Worcester plate, with nectarines on a mottled blue background, which would have quickened 'Chas.' Squibb's pulse.

Balfour's eyes were taken first by a Hollyer photograph of Olivia's mother and then the Sargent portrait of her, rather regal in yellow satin. It contrasted sharply with a photograph of Olivia, the only one that Balfour had ever seen, in which she was shown with another girl, both in their early teens, standing with linked arms on the terrace at Crabbe's Park. They wore white dresses, and fish-handled tennis racquets were propped by a cane chair. A click of the camera had magically caught the atmosphere of a long-ago summer evening. The looked as if they might have stopped there to exchange romantic confidences. With rather dreamy expressions they stared out into the parkland and the future.

Balfour picked up the Visitors' Book which had been started at Crabbe's Park in the year before Olivia's birth and finally petered out half a century afterwards at the outbreak of war in 1939. He flicked through the pages between 1905 and 1910, wondering which signature might belong to the other girl in the photograph. The book was full of minor divertissement. Bold aristocratic signatures which over the years became feeble, or shaky, and then disappeared – single appearances of composers – autographs of Press Barons which seemed to proclaim their fame and self-importance before they too went into the dark. As a postscript, made after the book, water-stained by firemen's hoses, had been retrieved from the ruined house, there was a quotation in Olivia's writing: 'Remembrances embellish life; forgetfulness alone makes it endurable.'

Another heavy volume lay by the Visitors' Book, an album bound in padded green morocco, badly scuffed and worn at the corners. Compiled by Olivia's mother, it consisted largely of photographs of 'Social Occasions' at Cliveden, Greystoke Castle, Crabbe's Park, Hagley Hall and Hatfield. With set smiles and in curiously unchanging attitudes the same people looked out from dozens of different backgrounds. There were snapshots of the famous hostesses Lady Desborough at Taplow Court and Mrs Arthur James at West Dean. A signed photograph of Queen Alexandra. 'Ships in Malta Harbour: Renown, Victorious, Ophir, Caesar . . .' Olivia was the sole surviving member of the Phelips and Malise families. When she died it was unlikely that anyone would want to preserve this relic of Edwardian and Imperial grandeur.

'Oh Ned!' The greeting seemed to have been carefully chosen to exclude warmth. Balfour turned to see Olivia standing in the doorway. She wore a dark blue brocaded silk suit and a white blouse with a high ruffed neck. Her skirt was a good deal longer than the present mode dictated, but otherwise her clothes seemed to be neither in nor out of fashion and impossible to date. She was only an inch or two shorter than Balfour and her face was thin, saved from severity by big grey eyes and a sensitive, sharply defined mouth. She had a high forehead and comely, simply dressed white hair. She waved a pamphlet at him as if she was irritated. 'I was surprised when you phoned yesterday. I thought Miss Bowyer said you would not return from Corsica till the end of the week?'

'That's what I planned. But I had to come back early as a friend of mine died, tragically. He fell from a building. Killed himself, I think. Mr Weiss – I'm sure I introduced him to you at that charity auction. The "Save the Children" fund evening.'

'Yes,' she said vaguely. 'I think I remember him. How terrible. I'm so sorry to hear that.'

He could see that she was disconcerted by this news but he could also tell that she did not want to hear of anything that would take her sympathy. Nevertheless her attitude relaxed a little. She put her hand on the handle of one of the french windows and said, 'Shall we go outside? I hate to waste even an hour of an afternoon like this. But perhaps you are sated with sun? I thought we might have tea out there.'

Balfour smiled and silently opened the window, struck by the briefness and poignancy of human relationships. There had been a hint of a quaver in Olivia's voice, an involuntary tremble of the larynx muscles, and in profile her face had a fragile quality that he had not noticed before. As he had been invited to tea it appeared that whatever he, or the firm of T. Edward Balfour, had done, the damage was not irreparable. But the trembling voice reminded him in an unpleasant nagging way that Olivia had a heart weakened by rheumatic fever. In a moment they would be standing outside the house as Olivia had stood with her friend outside Crabbe's Park, perhaps sixty years ago. Then that instant would be gone, as irrecoverable as the one shown in the photograph.

Olivia stopped on the miniature terrace, her thin hand resting on the low stone balustrade: 'I had a bad cold and was mewed-up in the house for nearly two weeks with only an occasional Pisgah-view. Since then I've had an absolute passion for being outside.'

As they went down the steps she tapped Balfour on the arm with the pamphlet she was carrying. 'For once that celebrated dealer T. Edward Balfour nodded.' There was humour not annoyance in the way she said this, so he was certain that this was not the cause for her coolness towards him. 'There was a Swinburne manuscript in a local sale. A draft of *Ave Atque Vale*, no less.'

'Really? I thought that was in the Eton College Library.'

'Yes, you're right, but this one is an earlier version with many of his alterations. Apparently in its travels it somehow reached a German collector who put it into a sumptuous black morocco case with his arms in gilt. While you were away it turned up for sale in Clapham!'

She handed Balfour the pamphlet. It was a catalogue issued by a firm of Estate Agents. A fairly typical production with too much information in small print crowded on to the front page: 'Messrs Haley & Coote Ltd will offer for Sale by Auction on Monday, 18th July, at 2.15 p.m. the Contents of "Eagle House", Cedars Road, Clapham Common, s w4. being Furniture & Effects, the property of the late Colonel F. K. Green, DSO, including Victorian, Modern & General Furniture, Oil Paintings, Antique flintlock guns, Pewter Percussion Cap guns . . .'

Balfour shook his head: 'A Swinburne manuscript among this lot?'

'Yes. And it wasn't even listed. Just included in some miscellaneous lots at the end. The whole thing is rather a mystery. A friend of mine who lives in Clapham Common North Side knew Colonel Green so she went along on the day the sale was advertised. Great confusion it seems, as there were crowds of dealers. The house was crammed with them . . .'

Balfour waved the catalogue. 'Crowds of dealers for this?' He had looked through it with an expert's eye, noting the inadequacy of the descriptions. It seemed to be a rather pedestrian collection and there was no mention of any autograph material. He subscribed to an agency which contracted to supply him with every auction catalogue mentioning letters or manuscripts, but they were not to blame in this case. 'I shouldn't have thought they would have turned out in strength.'

'Ah! That's where the mystery deepens. Apparently there were quite a number of interesting things. Some good pictures, silver, porcelain, mostly Continental, but all very badly described. By some means, however, the dealers congregated. And then the sale was postponed, on the Monday at 2.15 just when it was supposed to start. The auctioneer appeared on the dais and made a short statement to the effect that there was doubt about legal title to some of the items and the sale would have to be held after that had been cleared up. My friend says there was quite a shindig. Many dealers had come a long way. . . . Still it was fortunate from our point of view. The sale is now to be held tomorrow, 2.15 as before. Will you be able to go?'

'Of course. Delighted. How much do you want me to bid?'

'I shall leave it to you, but I should particularly like to have that fine poem for the collection.'

Balfour admired her attitude to collecting – she gave the impression of holding all her possessions lightly with open hands, and was detached even when being enthusiastic about some acquisition. She had once compared life and death to the playing of children on the sands. 'When you are very young the tide is so far out it seems that it will not come in again, and the children busy themselves with their sand-castles and walls of sand, but gradually they realize that it is returning and then it reaches them, remorselessly erasing every sign of their play. We are all just like children . . .'

They made a slow and thoughtful progress through the garden to the south side of the house. Balfour was sure that Olivia was formulating her approach to a difficult subject. They came to the walled court-yard where she grew peaches and sat by the goldfish pool. In the centre of the pool there were eighteenth-century figures of Cupid and Psyche, and the water gurgled in through the wide mouth of a leering satyr, a bronze effigy of a river-god which the copper carbonates of time had turned greenish-blue.

Olivia had an abstracted air and her face was slightly darkened by melancholy. When she swivelled round to face him Balfour knew that the climactic moment had come. 'Before I was imprisoned here by that cold I met Barbara and Toby by chance one day in London. What an adorable little boy! I was walking in Kensington Gardens and saw them by the Round Pond. Barbara asked me back for nursery tea. She told me that they had just come back from a holiday in the Scilly Isles, on Tresco ...' Olivia shook her head unbelievingly, moved by some far away emotion. 'I went there fifty-two years ago, on the 3rd August, 1914. How unreal it all seems now! That fateful date, the old steamer *Lyonesse* which took us there, the completely carefree mood we were in just a matter of hours before the holocaust was to begin. Even the clothes we wore then.' She turned to point at the house: 'My ancestor William Malise who built this house helped to provision Admiral Blake who captured Tresco from Sir John Granville for Cromwell. Our visit to that beautiful island seems just as far off and improbable somehow as Blake's. All phantoms ...'

Balfour heard her with growing unease. He knew that Olivia's fiancé had been killed at Mons and in other circumstances would have been interested to hear more of this trip to the Scillies which had never been mentioned before, but as soon as she had said Barbara's name he knew that it was his leaving Orme Square that lay beneath Olivia's changed attitude. He cursed himself for not having told her before – the telling would be no easier now and he had placed her in an embarrassing situation. But his reason for leaving Barbara, that after twenty years of marriage their relationship had become just a matter of indifference which Barbara did not seem to mind overmuch while he still needed the excitement and pleasure of being in love, was impossible to explain. When he had tried to talk about it to Sammy it had sounded absurd.

116

The only difference was that now he saw his quest for love as a delusion.

Olivia said: 'Toby took me into his room to see his toys. And all his particular treasures laid out on the window ledge. You remember that marvellous Patmore poem, "My little son, who look'd from thoughtful eyes" That serious little face as he talked to me then. Quite irresistible!' She put a frail-looking hand on Balfour's wrist: 'It's many years since I pried into anyone else's affairs and I didn't think I ever would again, but what is going to happen, Ned? Barbara was not explicit but I gathered you had moved to a flat in Bury Street. I remember so well you telling me you had lost your own parents when you were only five. Must the same kind of thing happen to Prudence and Toby?'

'I don't think so.' Balfour spoke without thinking his reply through to a definite conclusion, but he was not just producing a bromide to glide over the awkward question. It was an involuntary expression of what he had been feeling recently. Sammy had been right in saying that in a marriage the children did matter most, even from a selfish point of view. The words of the song, 'I want to be happy/But I can't be happy/Till I've made you happy too,' went round and round in his head – that summed up the position. Life with Barbara would never satisfy him but, as Sammy said, he would have to lump it. He had wanted a perfect woman companion but now he knew it was an illusion: marriage with Bunty would turn out in the end like marriage with Barbara. In pursuing the illusion he had found the reality to consist of trying, with dwindling success, to keep girls like Bunty amused or assuaging purely sexual desire with women like Mrs Alec Connolly. If Barbara would take him back it was a compromise at best, but it was one he wanted to make. Only that afternoon he had come a step closer to understanding himself: looking from Petersham Meadow down to Eelpie Island he had recognized that curve of the Thames as being the mysterious river scene which figured in his recurring halcyon dream. Revisiting that scene had induced a strange, varying emotion in him, it had been as if some previously unknown chord in his heart had been struck by accident, so that for a moment he had felt outside life and in the presence of the source of peace which the dream brought back to him. Now he knew that all his life the memory of an afternoon he had spent with his parents when he was three or four had been stored in his memory and formed a kind of sanctuary for him.

'I believe the black sheep may be taken back into the fold. I've learnt a lesson in the last few weeks. And I don't think Toby has really understood what has happened. With Prudence it's different of course . . .'

A very faint smile was shown only in the curving corners of Olivia's mouth. She nodded vehemently, urging on his confidence. 'Of course you can change things. You'll see – with Prudence. Life is an oxymel, a bitter-sweet thing at best, but its great gift is the possibility always for *change*. Any day while one is alive there is the chance of making a new start.'

Balfour said: 'I had the same advice from my friend Sam Weiss but then, alas, I was not in the mood to take it. And now he's dead, well I can't admit that I was wrong.'

'Don't let that thought weigh too much on you,' Olivia said quickly. 'You know, when I was a young girl I went to a fair at Stow and saw a grossly deformed man, a kind of human monster in an ill-lit booth. It was an image of pointless human misery that haunted me for years. But I did eventually learn from it – to concentrate my energies on what can be done, rather than brooding on things that cannot be remedied. Did Mr Weiss have a family?'

'He wasn't married. His only living relative is his sister who is a good deal older and I don't think she is in very good health. She lives in Tel Aviv. Sam asked me to be his executor and I shall have the job of seeing that his things are disposed of, I suppose. At least I can see that the pictures and books are sold to good advantage – half of everything he left is to go to the "Save the Children" fund.'

'He sounds very sympathetic to me. Now I regret that I didn't get a chance to talk to him at that auction. How odd life is – the people you see and could have known. To hear someone like that described ... There, you see, I'm indulging in useless regrets which I warned you against.' Olivia had a rueful expression. 'Poor Mr Weiss! Do you know why he killed himself?'

'No. And I don't think I ever shall now.'

15

'Was it an old party?' The taxi-driver had been talking in a confidential manner, through the side of his mouth, most of the way from Piccadilly. It had been quite interesting stuff, about how long it took to become a taxi-driver, how the trainee had to go round London on a bicycle for a year or more finding addresses and the best routes, but his voice was indistinct and Balfour had missed a certain amount of his confidences. Now Balfour leaned forward so that his head was near to the glass partition and asked, in a slightly amused voice: 'What party?' Though he had not heard all the conversation he did not see how it had got on to the subject of parties.

'The party you're going to see in Cedars Road, Clapham. I'm not just being nosey. All that area's been knocked practically flat for a council building scheme. It looks just like the City after the blitz.'

'I'm not going to see anyone. There's a sale of the contents of a house. Furniture, pictures, that kind of thing.'

'Ah, that explains it, you see. The council slapped compulsory purchase orders on all the houses that had to come down, but in a few cases where a very old party, eighty-odd say, was concerned they let them stay on as long as possible. I know that one or two houses were still there, scattered about. It's probably one of those old parties has popped off.'

'Eagle House, Cedars Road, Clapham Common. Property of the late Colonel F. K. Green, DSO,' Balfour read from the front of the catalogue.

'I know it. I know it all right.' The driver nodded vigorously. 'Whacking great eagles they are too. Stone ones.

Quite a big house, rather gloomy, Victorian – you know the kind of thing. Sticks out like a sore thumb now. It gives you rather a shock when you see it standing there and the rest razed. Looks as if it's survived the Bomb. As soon as we've crossed the Wandsworth Road you'll see it on the left. About the only one there I think, in that particular plot.'

Balfour looked at his watch and was surprised to find it was only 1.20. They had crossed the Chelsea Bridge and were making very good time in light traffic along the Queenstown Road. The sky was a uniform pale grey and the light rain looked as if it was set in for hours. He had spent the morning in his office examining the list of the collection of manuscripts in Ireland which Leo Spiegl had described – he had been surprised both to find it in his post and that Leo had not exaggerated the size and interest of the collection. It had taken him two hours to go through it with reasonable care. Then he had had an early lunch at the Vega Restaurant, the Imperial Salad with stuffed eggs, Gruyère cheese, asparagus tips and 'Sauce Piquante'. Now he was looking forward to the auction; he always enjoyed house sales more than those in the solemn atmosphere of the main London rooms, and this particular one looked as if it might be rather unusual and interesting. He had known other auctions when certain lots were withdrawn due to a query about the legal title, but it was rare for a whole sale to be postponed.

'There it is. Now I didn't exaggerate did I?'

Balfour looked along the road which was exactly as the taxi-driver had described it. For about a quarter of a mile all the houses had been demolished and the ground completely cleared, then one tall dark house loomed up. In a row of similar properties it would have appeared commonplace but alone it looked odd and forbidding. Everything about it was still intact – it was surrounded by a red brick wall about four feet high with a heavy spiked iron chain strung above it, the garden contained several straggly lilac bushes, and a Monkey Puzzle tree grew too near the front door. Lace curtains covered all the windows and added to the atmosphere of secrecy – it was easy to imagine a chronic invalid leading a recluse's existence there. There was a row of cars parked along the curb in front of the house and more of them filled the semi-circular drive.

When the taxi stopped Balfour noticed that the driver was engrossed in watching something in his mirror. 'That's funny,' he said. 'You look back there, guv. See that light blue car – the Ford Galaxie? That's followed us all the way here – I noticed it first in Sloane Street. Powerful job that, you know. Six-litre engine. Could have passed us zoom, but it didn't. Now we've stopped and heigh presto it's stopped too! And there's nothing to stop for, right?'

Balfour wheeled round and saw the big blue car was being backed off the road. As the taxi-man had pointed out, there was no reason why it should stop there, half-way along the cleared site. He watched it move forward into the road again and then turn back the way it had come. After he had paid the taxi-driver and seen him U-turn to follow the Galaxie, Balfour remembered that Squibb had said Victor Maddox owned 'a big, baby-blue American car'. It seemed possible that the Maddox gang might still be watching him to see if he was 'nosing into' their affairs, and he was glad that a visit to a house sale at Clapham must surely appear innocent enough from their point of view.

Several men were leaving the house and one of them was having difficulty extricating his car from the queue in the drive: there was not much room and he had to do a good deal of jockeying backwards and forwards. 'What a game,' he called out to Balfour, 'and all for nowt!'

Ignoring the rain Balfour stood for a moment looking at the stone eagles, which were badly eroded and practically black, and then at the house. The topography conformed roughly to his nightmare when he had been searching an old house from room to room, although this one was larger. At one time no doubt it had looked quite grand, but it had obviously been left without repairs in recent years and the brick-work badly needed re-pointing. Water was gushing down one wall from a stopped-up gutter. There was a smell of drains.

When he approached the front door Balfour realized he was being watched by two men who were hesitating beneath the tiled porch as if undecided whether to brave the rain. One man held his nose and then made a movement to pull an imaginary lavatory chain. Balfour recognized him as a silver dealer he had met at various country sales. The man grimaced at him with an expression of mixed humour and bitterness: 'You're wasting your time, old cock. All the good stuff's gone.'

Balfour looked at his watch: 'Really? Surely the sale doesn't start for three-quarters of an hour yet?'

'No, you misunderstand me, laddie. They've whipped the right goods and left the crap. The bastards. It's a right balls-up.' His fat companion who had a rich air of fraudulence about him, as if his smart clothes had been hired from a theatrical store as part of a confidence trick, extended a curiously symmetrical hand, like a flesh-coloured starfish, to point at Balfour's catalogue. 'That's out of date now. Been replaced by this. And believe me mate, you're welcome to it.' He handed Balfour a duplicated list. 'All the silver's gone. And the Meissen. The singing bird boxes. It stinks! Messrs Haley & Coote haven't heard the last ...' He strode off into the rain making empty threats.

The silver dealer remained and said to Balfour: 'Still, you might as well go in. There's a free buffet of sorts. Good German wine. Ad lib if you like that sort of thing.'

The inside of the house was a good deal gloomier than Balfour had expected. The large lilac bushes obscured the windows, and the walls of the hall were covered with a paper imitation of dark oak panelling. A small, high electric bulb's glow extended only a few feet. But despite the dim light and the faintly depressing atmosphere there was plenty of spirited conversation and laughter going on somewhere. Gradually he tracked it down to the back of the hall. There was a hubbub of voices, glasses clinking and the occasional pop of a bottle being opened. The imitation oak panelling was covered with dusty spears, shields and swords all hopefully looped with lot numbers. Halfway along the hall a tall man with a stony expression was fiddling with an ancient cabinet gramophone: he was playing a scratched record of Jeannette Macdonald singing *Lover come back to me* but by altering the speed switch he was making her sound alternatively like Minnie Mouse and a lugubrious bass. As Balfour walked past he saw that the man was playing another game, sprinkling needles on the spinning record so that they were flung off. An empty Moselle bottle and a tumbler stood on the floor by his feet.

Balfour opened the door to find himself in a large old-fashioned kitchen crowded with people gaily chattering as if a cocktail party was being held there. On a bare scrubbed table there were some plates of sandwiches backed by a row of Moselle and Hock bottles. He dusted a tumbler with a paper napkin and quickly downed two glasses from a Moselle bottle on which the paper label was so damp-stained as to be illegible.

'Hi, Ned!' Balfour looked round to see Maurice Erskine, an American book-dealer who spent as much time in London as he did in New York. Silver-haired, immaculate, urbane, he drifted nonchalantly through the world apparently to better effect than most of those who worked ten hours a day: business for him was usually conducted over dining-tables or at parties from which he emerged with an author's archive or the entrée to a ducal library. His lips were ironically compressed as if he wanted not to smile too obviously. 'Ha-ha, I feel much better seeing you fell into the same elephant trap. But whisper it not in New Bond Street that we've been had. Secret. However the wine's not bad and the price is right.' He proferred a cobwebbed bottle. 'Some of the wine was withdrawn from the sale too, but the porters had very ingeniously stood a lot of bottles upright and they were described as spoilt and left to console the frustrated – us. So be my guest. Ah drink up the bitter cup of discontent. Is that bad Omar or did I make it up?' He slopped wine into Balfour's already half-full glass so that it ran over at the brim. 'There we are. If this failing palate does not deceive me, a rareish vintage from the old Wurttenberg estates, *Weingut Graf Metternich*. Yes, whoever liberated this had taste – or luck. But I have taste.'

Balfour drank the mixture of wines greedily. It should not have been good, and probably would not have been to a connoisseur, but he enjoyed it. He felt rather frustrated as it seemed probable that the Swinburne manuscript had been withdrawn with the other interesting items, and the odd situation made him feel like drinking a lot. The supply did appear to be unlimited. 'Liberated? What you mean liberated?' He slurred his words deliberately but knew that he would soon be feeling light-headed and was looking forward to it.

Maurice Erskine took his cue and leant forward slightly in a mock drunk stance. 'I mean just simply liberated, old mansh. You were in the army, didn't you ever liberate anything, a camera or some such unwanted trifle? Why, it was rumoured that some of my GI brothers-in-arms even carried pincers to "liberate" gold fillings from corpses.'

Balfour frowned: 'You mean old Colonel Green looted this stuff?'

Erskine shook his head: 'No, I don't think so; I'm told the Colonel was crippled in the First World War and the *disiecta membra* we are mourning quite plainly came out of Germany in the 44/45 campaign. But why am I having to tell you all this – weren't you here in July when this crazy affair was first hatched?'

'No, I was in Corsica on vacation.'

'Ah, well you missed some fun. You see it appears the more interesting stuff was found crated up in cellars and added rather as an after-thought. Ludicrously underdescribed. The harpy, officially the Colonel's housekeeper but some say mistress, to whom the old boy left the stuff, was overjoyed at the idea of extra cash and careful not to inquire from whence it had come. She did not know what the word provenance meant, let alone care about it. So on 18th July we were all running around like mad guys, making wonderful discoveries. Excuse the cliché but it was like being set free in Aladdin's cave – well a mini-Aladdin's ... I came across those manuscripts, all beautifully done up in black morocco cases. But they've been taken out too, so you've no need to be so cagey, Ned.'

Balfour reached for another bottle. 'It certainly is rather a swindle. I shall have to do some serious thinking to recoup my expenses.'

Erskine said quietly: 'Yes, but do find time to pop up and have a look at the old Colonel. His portrait I mean, on the landing. Tell me if it doesn't remind you of a mutual customer. In the meantime I'm going to prime the fool auctioneer and get the rest of the story. There's some dark secret here and I'm rather hooked on it. You see that pompous little man, that's the famous Mr Stanley Coote – he'll tell me all before I'm finished.' He moved off brandishing a bottle like a weapon at a small dapper man, with a flushed complexion, who had been nodding portentously through a young woman's conversation and now said: 'Agreed it is an *ad hoc* situation, but I think we are coping.'

Balfour went back along the ill-lit hall. Through an open door on his right he could see that a large room had been prepared for the sale with rows of chairs set round a table covered with a green baize cloth. The joker with the gramophone was playing *If I had a talking picture of you* but had again slowed the speed down so much that the singer uttering 'you-ou-ou' sounded in great pain. The joker said benignly 'Picturesquissima, eh?' pointing at the stuffed animal heads which were displayed on the wall leading upstairs. The art of taxidermy was the one Balfour rated lowest, but the grotesque collection did exert a strange fascination as he went slowly upwards. There was strong smell of dust and decay; a stifling atmosphere of stagnation. It seemed impossible that anyone would want these literally moth-eaten relics. He noticed that a glass eye was hanging down from an empty socket in a tiger's head and tried to push it back, but only succeeded in starting a steady trickle of sawdust.

Along the corridor at the top of the stairs the unattractive animal exhibits were replaced by a few large and unfashionable paintings. Midway there was a portrait without a lot number. A skilful oils lettered on the heavy gilt frame: 'Colonel F. K. Green, DSO', showing a handsome, well-fed face with full wings of grey hair under the dark blue dress cap. The first impression was flattering – Balfour felt that in reality the light blue eyes could not have been so large nor the complexion quite so clear, the eyebrows perfectly arched and diminishing down to points as if they had been plucked. But studying the painting Balfour felt that the artist's attitude to his sitter had been ambivalent. It was a clever study which no doubt had pleased the Colonel and yet hinted at a not altogether favourable impression of his character. The grey moustache was meticulously trimmed to frame a small 'rosebud' mouth that was faintly epicene: some masterly touch had achieved a nuance of depravity in the bold soldier-like stare from periwinkle-coloured eyes.

'Ned! Kiddo!' Balfour had taken a step backwards to further appraise the portrait and was standing pressed against the banisters. He turned round on hearing his name to see Leo Spiegl at the bottom of the stairs. Spiegl exclaimed 'Say, this must be the place!' in a theatrically loud voice. He was dressed in a navy blazer with brass buttons, pale grey cotton trousers, navy tie decorated with gold chess castles, white buckskin shoes and a straw fedora with a snap brim and wide navy ribbon. He looked and sounded as if he should be on stage opening a musical comedy and for a moment Balfour half expected a chorus line to trot out from one of the doors in the hall.

'That's a joke but seriously this *is* the place,' Spiegl explained coming up the stairs. 'Knowl Green – remember? You worried me with it, how Mr Weiss had left a list with *my* name and Knowl Green. We-ell.' He pointed to the portrait. 'Mr Ned Balfour, may I introduce Colonel Frederick Knollys Green. You see!'

'You're sure about this?' Balfour queried, his slightly bemused mind trying to deal with the jumble of the possibilities contained in this pregnant sentence.

'One hundred per cent. It's too close to be a coincidence. Look. You tell me that Mr Weiss has died leaving a list with my name on it. Naturally I'm worried. It's an eerie feeling, not knowing why. How would you like it? But you fooled me by saying that the other name was definitely a place, Knowl Green. I knew I'd never been to it. Then I remember this sale. And this is the clincher – Mr Weiss was here. I hardly said a word to him, I was in too much of a hurry, running round looking at all the goodies and sizing up the opposition, then deciding on my marks for the sale. But he *was* here.'

'You still don't remember anything to do with the other names on the list, Steiner and Quarry?'

'Absolutely not. And I don't know why he should have put my name down. Unless, it's just possible, he wanted to ask me something about the sale. But if so, then what? I've been puzzled about that. Let's face it. Mr Weiss was an amateur but he knew as much as I do. What could I tell him?'

Balfour caught sight of his own reflection in a dark tarnished mirror – he had a hungry 'Bisto Kids' expression. With one sentence Spiegl had upset his theory about Sammy's death: it was as if he had been working on a crossword puzzle but had got a key-word wrong. Sammy had been seen brooding on a list of names and two of them were linked with this aborted sale. Did the other names stem from it as well, and the TERRIBLE DECISION?

'On a purnt of order, Mr Chairman.' Maurice Erskine was ascending the stairs, holding a bottle and a glass, doing his sinisterly accurate Senator McCarthy imitation. 'If I may be allowed just one word here. I have the complete inside story.' He took a good swig of wine then continued in McCarthy's wearing, declamatory voice. 'Gentlemen.

This is indeed potent stuff, and I mean the scandal not the vino. I've just had all my suspicions confirmed by Mr Stanley Coote, well-loved auctioneer and fool entrepreneur. The "liberated" goods which added so much spice to this sale were it seems sent to Colonel Green, suh, by his son, also a member of the licentious soldiery, in 1945. Apparently they were on buddy-buddy terms at that time and the old man was not above harbouring stuff looted from the Krauts. Then, it appears, they had a real bust-up. Possibly something to do with the housekeeper who by then was sharing the Colonel's bed? Anyway the split was final and the son even changed his name. The goods were left behind – perhaps they were the Colonel's share of the proceeds? But when the sale was announced the son sent in his spies. Followed great activity behind the scenes. Son now very wealthy, prominent figure, extremely reluctant to be connected with these pillaged goodies and his solicitors therefore arrange they should be withdrawn on payment of an adequate, nay generous sum. And so gentlemen we are left with a sale in which the high-spots are the Colonel's honest possessions, such as a Fred Sandys painting and a Binetto cabinet reed organ. He shook his head sadly and put a smeared wine-glass on a dark red plush chair. Christ, I could do with both a cuppa coffee and a leak. Can such things be?'

Leo Spiegl was obviously excited by these revelations. 'So it's true these things were knocked off? Rumours – well, a suggestion – of this I heard before but to have it confirmed rocks me. How could it happen?' He directed a slightly malicious glance at Balfour: 'Were the Britishers allowed to loot? How else could they bring back all that booty?'

Erskine answered him: 'Don't fool yourself, Leo. It wasn't a British monopoly. I was in Bad Salzemen, Magdeburg and Shonebeck in April '45 and saw plenty of "souvenirs" being taken by GIs. We had just heard about concentration camps like Ohrdruf, overrun by the Third Army under Patton. And don't forget, we'd taken plenty of crap from the Krauts for nine months. I picked up some Zeiss binoculars in a pile of rubble in Barby. Do you think I went out and posted up a found notice? Believe me, to take a lot of Kraut goods then only two things were necessary – to be up front pronto after the fire-fights and to have transport. But I still haven't come to the crunch of Mr Stanley Coote's indiscreet confidences. Do you know who the Colonel's "liberating" son turns out to be? Did you get the clue from the Colonel's portrait?'

Balfour said, 'No. An interesting face but it didn't remind me of anyone.'

'No resemblance to a noted man about town, a celebrated collector of all things beautiful? A rather opulent figure who drives a white Lamborghini Miura and has a Baglietto motor yacht at Cannes?'

Balfour shook his head with a wry expression: 'This just shows we move in two different worlds.'

Erskine was reluctant to stop the game. He tried another clue as though convinced that Balfour and Spiegl could guess if they would only make more effort. 'Flashes a fabulous Patek Phillippe watch.' The wine he had drunk gave him some trouble with 'fabulous Patek' and he paused as though he was saying it over again in his mind. 'No? Pity. More of a punch line if you knew him. Ah well – in 1945 the Colonel's son was a comparatively humble Captain L. K. Green of His Majesty's Army. Today none other than Mr Leonard K. G. Cato, captain of industry and financier extraordinary. It seems that after the bust-up he took his mother's name . . .'

The denouement had a riveting effect on Balfour but hardly less on Spiegl – through the long anecdote and questions he had barely been able to contain his impatience. At one point he had deftly tweezered a long black hair from his right nostril as if unaware of what he was doing and then sneezed explosively. Now he banged Erskine's arm to show that enough had been said. 'What a pay off! The joker in the pack,' he said excitedly. 'A phoney. Through and through.' He nudged Balfour:

'Didn't I tell you? Too big a man to see me, eh!' He whistled significantly in a way which augured ill for Cato's future reputation.

Erskine raised his eyebrows and asked Balfour: 'So you do know Cato then?'

'Only by name. Never seen him as far as I know. Certainly never had any dealings with him. But by an odd coincidence Leo was telling me only the other day that he'd tried without success to see Mr Cato at his impressive set-up in the City.'

Balfour felt incompetent to deal with this latest bit of information. Apart from the slightly numbing effect of the wine, it did not seem to fit into the puzzle. Finding that 'Knowl Green' did mean something had led him to believe that he might discover the other names on the list and their significance for Weiss, but Cato's 'crime' of war-time looting seemed to be a dead-end. While Sam would have been interested to see the things that had come from Nazi Germany, it was very unlikely that he would have felt concerned about it – not while he still had deformed fingers and nails to remind him that he had once been strung up in chains for six hours at the whim of SS *Oberführer* Lorritz.

Spiegl nodded sagely, as if some inward discussion had been brought to a satisfactory conclusion, then chuckled. 'I had this queer dream about Mr Leonard Cato. Mixed up with that damn big clock they made me sit under. Cato – it was very queer 'cos I knew him but I'd never seen him – came to me on his knees and pleaded for forgiveness. On his knees yet.' His bright pink tongue flickered out to touch his full lips and his eyes looked like shiny black stones. 'And there's the funny part. It could come true.'

The three men made their way slowly down the dark stairs. The joker in the hall had stopped fiddling with the gramophone and had set the cabinet reed organ in motion. Hesitantly, with long pauses during which it seemed to fail and recover, it played a faint rendering of *The last rose of summer*. It was an appropriate farewell performance

131

on these old premises which would soon be demolished. The plaintive, wavering tune captured their attention for a moment and they stood in silence. Balfour looked at the other two and wondered if they were experiencing the same sensation of the impermanence of all things human.

The door to the large room opened and the deeply flushed face of Mr Stanley Coote appeared. He gestured disapprovingly at the Binetto organ: 'That must be the last number I'm afraid. By request. A very valuable piece that, and the sale will be starting soon anyway.' He opened the door wider to show the chairs set out round the green-covered table. 'You see. We've made it look just like Sotheby's for you, gentlemen.' They ignored him and went on towards the continuing sounds of celebration coming from the kitchen.

Spiegl put his hand on Balfour's arm. 'See that small door? Steep steps down to the cellars. Now that's where I saw Mr Weiss. Dashed down and up again in a few minutes. There were stacks of wine bottles and a few oddments, but mostly rubbish in wooden crates. Yes, Mr Weiss was definitely down there. Just let me think. With some dealers. Old nut-case Henry Parfitt was one of them.'

'Our 'enry 'ere on 18th July?' Erskine queried in a poor attempt at Cockney. 'Well I didn't see him. Boy! I bet his heart was broken when the sale was called off. But you see he's too wide to appear today. Got a tip-off I suppose. Crafty old sod. You know, I think I can truly say I've had a fair amount of experience in the funny old book world but 'enry Parfitt H'esquire is the only real bibliomaniac I've ever met. Just can't imagine him doing anything besides gloat over books. Yet he must sleep and eat and drink I guess. Speaking of drink . . .'

16

BOOKS BOUGHT. A newly painted sign twelve inches high dominated Henry Parfitt's bookshop in Market Row off the Clerkenwell Road. At the edge of a long decaying area the Row had once again become a busy thoroughfare and several of the shops had been, as Parfitt ruefully put it, 'tarted up'. But his own premises still looked as if they had not been touched since they had suffered the effects of shock from a nearby flying bomb in 1944. It was rumoured that he had refused free repairs from the bomb damage people because he feared that the whole ramshackle premises, groaning under tons of books, might come tumbling down. The peeling black paint of his façade and the window full of dusty calf-bound volumes contrasted sharply with the Ionian white and gold of his neighbour's china shop, but the sign BOOKS BOUGHT was touched up regularly. The buying of books as opposed to selling was the important part of business as far as Parfitt was concerned. He had told Balfour that he lived in hopes of 'some old lady from the Shires spotting that sign. She'll come toddling in one day, you'll see. Just been left this whacking great library of folios but knows nothing about 'em. So she'll need 'elp.'

When Balfour reached Market Row from Clapham it was nearly five o'clock. The light rain of the early afternoon had given place to a cold downpour and the sky was so dark it was hard to believe it was August and that in Calvi Bunty would still be broiling under a harsh sun. It was the kind of day when there appears to be a definite demonstration of how frail and brief summer's hold is in England.

Balfour approached the shop aware that a cocoon of self-consciousness was already forming about him. He had little in common with Parfitt and always felt completely artificial in his presence, projecting the false persona of someone anxious to learn from the noted cockney scholar/bookseller. Parfitt knew a fantastic amount about books and could have been quite interesting, but insisted always in putting his patter over in a series of rhetorical questions, interspersed with a good deal of complaining about how difficult it was to find worthwhile books.

When the door was opened Balfour stood still, faintly amused by the thought that he was under surveillance from the back room – if a suspicious character entered the shop Parfitt would scuttle across the floor at alarming speed to protect his stock. Balfour peered at the undusted shelves which went right up to the ceiling. The top ones contained out-of-date Whitaker's Almanacks, children's encyclopedias, histories of the 1914–18 War and other large tomes which were not touched from one year to another. Parfitt earned enough to live by selling novels to librarians and hiring out bindings to theatres and film studios – he hived off any valuable books into the rabbit warren of odd-shaped rooms above where he lived with his ancient mother in miserly surroundings.

Parfitt made a ghost-like, silent appearance in the archway which led to his cluttered back room. He was thin and had a chalk-white face, long black hair, dark brown eyes and lashes which looked as if they had been made up or touched with coal dust. Dark patches under his eyes accentuated his resemblance to the silent film comedian Larry Semon.

'Just been along to Cedars Road.' Balfour often bought autograph letters from Parfitt but always felt compelled to give a reason for calling at the shop. 'I heard you were there last month. Thought I'd let you know you didn't miss anything by not turning out again. You were very wise not to bother. All the books and manuscripts were withdrawn.'

Parfitt grinned knowingly to show that this outcome had been foreseen, and patted himself all over until he doggedly discovered a packet of cigarettes. He lit one and began to smoke in a way which made it look like an experimental process – holding it in stiff fingers at arm's length between puffs. He brooded with satisfaction on Balfour's admission of defeat and then began to speak in a slow, self-important voice which had led to Spiegl referring to him as "is bumship the Mayor'. He dealt, as always, arbitrarily with the letter 'h': 'Yes, but you'd agree, wouldn't you, that h'it's only part of the general shortage of good stuff. H'it's just bloody typical of the trend today.' When he was not asking rhetorical questions Parfitt's statements were masked by a dubitative tone, but he was as quick on his mental feet as he was in covering possible shop-lifters. His dark eyes flickered over Balfour's face and he said 'Great pity about Mr Weiss. H'it shook me h'I can tell you. Terrible. H'awful. Tragic . . .'

He stopped heaping on adjectives and shot Balfour a shrewd, judging look to see if he had been sympathetic enough and could get back, with relief, to the only subject that really interested him. Balfour was reminded of a sentence which Max Weber was fond of quoting: 'Life has no moral, and the moral of art is that life is worthwhile without one'; life without a moral or any eternal significance was worthwhile for Balfour but art alone could not make it so, and he was out of sympathy with that view. Pictorial art was all-important for Max, Henry Parfitt was obsessed with books – while he might occasionally envy their great enthusiasms, Balfour found such single-mindedness bearable only in small doses.

'Did you talk to Sam at the sale?' Balfour asked. 'I was wondering what it was that interested him there.'

'Didn't have a chance really. You know, h'I'm sure, that the catalogue was well and truly a compendium of h'errors. That Mr Coote, 'e didn't know a book from 'is h'elbow. No, I saw Mr Weiss only for a moment, down in the cellar; 'e was rooting around there most of the time I think but I was very busy elsewhere. H'and all to no avail. What a farce h'it was ...'

Some sound unheard by Balfour had attracted Parfitt's attention and he broke off to move to the book-stacked stairs which led to ill-lit rooms above: 'NOT YET, MOTHER,' he shouted. There was a muttered reply and he said, 'H'I can't come now, mother. Not for ten minutes at least,' in a tart tone that made plain his irritation.

'Mother,' he said in explanation to Balfour. 'Percy was with me,' he added vaguely. 'H'if you can spare a minute pop down and 'ave a word with 'im. H'it might be worthwhile. 'E stayed down with Mr Weiss in the cellar at Cedars Road while I was 'untin' out the h'incunabula.'

'Well, I think I will,' Balfour said, moving to the well of the iron corkscrew staircase which led down to the basement where Parfitt's old assistant Percy Dixon usually worked. 'Is he down there? There's no light.'

'Ho yes, 'e's there all right. Having a little nap you know. 'E does when 'e's finished the parcels, and dustin' and sortin'. Well why not?'

Balfour waited at the top of the tortuous staircase until Parfitt rather reluctantly switched on the light in the basement. It was a narrow, cramping method of descent and one had to duck hastily at the bottom as the last step brought one immediately to a low doorway.

Percy Dixon was revealed asleep with mouth agape in a deck-chair between piles of books. He wore a black suit jacket with mole-coloured broad-waled corduroy trousers. A bowler hat was on a hook with his raincoat and grey apron. On the floor by his chair there was an emptied mug of tea and a tiny crumpled paper bag. A crumb of biscuit trembled on his Bruce Bairnsfather moustache. Balfour liked Percy Dixon and knew something of his life – that the highpoint of it appeared to be his time in the army in 1914–17, that he now lived with a sister in Islington, that his lunch always consisted of two sandwiches, one of Marmite and one of marmalade – and had once witnessed the old man's difficult yet shameless tears over the death of his dog. Percy's temperament was keyed low – it was as if he had been trounced by life and no longer had any expectations.

Balfour waited silently, glancing at the top volume of a tottering pile of bound numbers of *The Boy's Own Paper*, not wishing to waken the old man. A loudly ticking kitchen alarm clock accentuated the passing of time and the lonely tedious hours Percy spent there. Suddenly he gave an incensed grunt as if a dream had ended unsatisfactorily, cautiously opened a blood-shot eye, and vigorously smoothed his quiff of iron-grey hair.

'Hullo Mr Balfour. Nice to see you. Quite a stranger ...' He paused and shot a suspicious glance in the direction of the staircase. 'Has that old toe-rag been going on about me again? He was blowing me up about the ablutaries. I arst you, what can I do. All the brick-work's sodden and crumbling there. And dirt! It's like the Black Hole of Calcutta. Going on at me just because some posh American librarian was taken short here yesterday.'

Balfour had once had to use the dark, evil-smelling 'ablutaries' and sympathized about the daunting nature of keeping them clean. 'No, Percy. He's forgotten that by now. And he knows you do your work properly. I only wanted to inquire if you enjoyed your little outing to Clapham. The mystery sale that was postponed.'

Percy muttered something defensively as if he could not quite accept the rapid change of topic, but after a moment his eyes twinkled. 'Oh yes. Coo we had a right time there. What a caper! Nobody knew what was what. And the porters had opened some bottles of the old vin blank. Everyone scurrying about in a right tizz-was. Meself, I stayed in the cellar and polished off most of a bottle.' Some obtrusive thought had plainly occurred to him – he tugged at a large wax-like ear and moved uneasily in his chair. 'That was a real tragedy about your friend, poor little Mr Weiss. A really nice bloke. One of the old school.'

'I was going to ask you about him. I wondered if he

was on to something good in the cellar. Mr Parfitt and Leo Spiegl both said they had seen him busy down there. Did you spot anything unusual?'

'No. . . . Not specially. . . . Not that I noticed.' Percy did not look at Balfour so that his heavy dull face seemed somehow eyeless. There were gaps of strange silence and Balfour had the distinct impression that there was something Percy was reluctant to mention but was encountering in thinking about the sale. He pressed on with his questions, ruthless about the old man's feelings in his keenness to make a discovery. 'You did see something, didn't you? I should be very grateful, Percy, if you'd tell me. Believe me, it's not just idle curiosity. Mr Weiss was a very good friend of mine and I've been trying to find out what he was doing while I was away – anything which might have led up to . . .'

Percy sat perfectly still, leaning slightly forward in the deck-chair, his face expressionless so that Balfour wondered if he might not have taken in the rapid sentences or if he was suffering from asphasia. There was a long awkward silence then Percy sniffed, said quietly, 'Trouble is,' and then, 'Has you-know-who said anything about you-know-what?' He indicated the stairs with a stiff inclination of his head.

'Nothing. He was too busy looking at the incunabula.'

'Good. I'm not really surprised because he doesn't take in much about other people, but he did pop down just – at a crucial moment and told me to gee-up, so I wondered . . . I can tell you I've been very puzzled about this, Mr Balfour. And I wouldn't mention it to anybody else. . . . There was a big portfolio of drawings laid out on a table in the cellar, you see. And Mr Weiss and another man I didn't know got very excited about some of those drawings. They were gabbling away about them in German so of course I couldn't understand, but their expressions were enough. Then – this is the real mystery. There were quite a few wooden crates full of odds and ends you see – all the personal stuff which was not included in the sale.

The porters said the old girl, the housekeeper, a hard piece apparently, had sorted out anything that had no commercial value and it was all going to be taken away by the dustmen. Well, Mr Weiss and this other chap started looking through these boxes. Fair enough that, I suppose. But – I saw Mr Weiss pocket some of the papers. Shook me that did.'

'You mean Mr Weiss stole something? You're sure, because it would really be stealing if he took something from the house, worthless or not. That doesn't sound like him.'

Percy winced slightly at Balfour's sharp tone in response to the confidence, then said, 'Do me a favour. 'Course I'm sure,' in a peevish voice that implied he was tired of attacks on his failing powers. 'I was just sitting in a corner with this bottle so I suppose they thought I had passed out or wouldn't notice. But I saw Mr Weiss take a photograph. And some letters or papers.' His false teeth clicked lightly over labials and he moved them into position with his tongue before he said vehemently: 'On a stack of bibles! He slipped them into his pocket when he thought no one was looking. I couldn't understand it then no more than you can believe it now.'

*

Sam Weiss's house, No. 1 Paley Street, was crowded in at the end where it joined Cheyne Walk. A very narrow house, unlike its neighbours, it looked as if it had been added as an afterthought or had survived from an earlier row. Balfour walked boldly up to the front door and opened it with a key which had been in his possession since the previous year when Sammy had spent a long holiday in Israel.

Despite his bold approach Balfour was experiencing an unpleasant mixture of apprehension and guilt which became much worse once the door closed behind him. His right to enter the house was very doubtful even though he was the sole executor, but apart from the surreptitious entry of premises locked up by the police the atmosphere in the hall was strange and faintly repugnant to him. The white vinyl walls glistened with damp – being so near to the river the house required a daily airing – and there was an unpleasant stale odour, but it was the silence that was eerie and disconcerting. He stood quite still, straining to hear any voices that might come from the upper floors – he had the illogical conviction that at any moment the silence could be broken by Sammy playing something by Schumann on his cherished Bechstein, putting on a Duparc record, or appearing at the head of the stairs humming *Mondnacht*.

Balfour's instinct was to turn on his heel and leave the house, but his always strong sense of curiosity had been fed by the odd Cedars Road set-up and the revelation that Sammy had taken some papers from the cellar. It seemed certain that the names on the list Garratt had remembered did link up somehow, but their connection with Knollys Green tended to demolish his previous theory about a smuggling ring. He could not believe it was possible that Leonard Cato's looting incident in 1945 led on to the Victor Maddox gang in 1966, but he still wanted to see if he could find the papers stolen from Cedars Road. He knew the Paley Street house as well as his own flat and he could make a much more effective search than any policeman.

Balfour glanced quickly round the kitchen, sitting-room and the small dining alcove. There was a pile of unopened newspapers and a bottle of Eggnog on the kitchen table, otherwise everything seemed to be in its usual place.

It was on the second floor that Sammy had spent most of his time. The largest room in the house was practically bare of furniture but it contained a few prized paintings, the Bechstein, an elaborate hi-fi apparatus and a very large collection of records in specially made cupboards. Balfour entered it just for a brief look round with a strong feeling that he was intruding, then went into the smaller book-lined room which looked out on to Paley

Street. Apart from housing most of Sammy's books, there were niches for a Renaissance green marble torso and a rare twelfth-century Khmer Buddha. From the window Balfour had a narrow, oblique view of the rain-drenched Gardens which shielded Cheyne Walk from the incessant traffic along the Embankment, and the top half of the Carlyle statue.

All the papers in Sammy's desk had been taken from the drawers and now stood in neat piles together with cheque stubs done up in bundles, old bills and letters. A few pages torn from an exercise book were held in place by a piece of incense-stained marble, glowing like tortoise-shell. They were notes Sammy had made about Dachau, beginning: 'Some notable men in Dachau while I was there: General Werkmann, formerly secretary to Emperor Charles; Prince Ernest and Prince Max of Hohenberg (sons of Archduke Francis Ferdinand); the former consul-general Kleinwachter ...' Sammy had often talked of writing something about his experiences in Dachau, so Balfour was not surprised to come across these rather disjointed jottings which jumped from names of the *Schutz-Staffe* guards such as Lorritz, Kogl and Wagner to 'some men wore armlets inscribed *Blod* (idiots)', but he was puzzled to find a page in another hand headed: 'Buchenwald. Near Weimar is Ettersberg where there once was a beautiful beech-wood – Buchenwald. Inscribed on the gate at the camp: "My country, right or wrong" ...' At the top of this page Sammy had scrawled in red ink: 'Buchenwald. Check with Hermann Roth. April 1945.' Balfour had never heard of Roth but he did know that Sammy had not been in Buchenwald and thought it odd that he should be querying something that had happened there twenty years ago. He was struck once again by the difficulty of making sense of a dead man's private affairs and papers. If he could not do it, what chance did Superintendent Hanson have?

There were two photographs on the desk. One was a silver-framed snapshot of the Weiss family taken in

Vienna in 1913. It showed Sammy as a small child held up in his father's arms in a shadowy square in front of a church; it was inscribed in red ink on the back 'Franziskanerplatz'. Of the seven people shown there, three had left Austria before 1939 but Sammy's other two sisters and both his parents had stayed behind to find death in Auschwitz, the extermination camp. Small wonder that Sammy's bitterness about the Nazis had not abated at all with the passage of years, and that he was still liable to demolish arguments about their culpability by quoting the words *'Reines Juden Fett'* that had actually been engraved on bars of soap. He did not bother to mention that he had once been thrown in a latrine at Dachau, and suspended from a chain so that his feet did not touch the ground. 'Pure Jewish lard' was enough.

The other photograph had been torn from a magazine. It showed a line of Jewish children led by a boy of about eight in clothes that were too big for him. They were being shepherded along against a background of barbed wire by Black Guards armed with sub-machine guns. The faces of the children seemed to be mainly eyes. Great dark eyes with haunting expressions. This was what it was all about. The photograph by itself refuted Olivia Phelips' theory that war could never be justified.

Balfour slowly ascended the stairs to the third floor. He was continuing the search mechanically but it seemed as pointless as his feelings of guilt about the Jewish children. Weird and irrelevant ideas flooded his mind then left him in a depressed and tired mood. He stood by the window in the main bedroom which was covered by white Venetian blinds, looking at the dismal streets and car lights on Battersea Bridge, hardly aware of where he was. He fingered the blinds as if they were bars on a cell window: they had been fitted to shield Sam from the vertiginous view. He regarded the far prospect of the grey river, then glanced quickly down to the greasy pavement to induce the feeling of falling. Oscar Wilde had written, 'It is what we fear that happens to us.' If Sammy had indeed killed himself, how desperate he must have been to face death in an aspect that so terrified him.

Balfour picked up some old-fashioned jointed shoe-trees and reluctantly opened a wardrobe to put them away. He intensely disliked the idea that he would have to deal with all of Sammy's personal belongings. On a small bed-side table he saw there was a pile of books and some more notes on odd scraps of paper. Most of the jottings were trivial day-to-day memoranda, but it gave him a curious shock to come across his own name written on the back of an invitation to a Cork Street art gallery: 'Ned. Part adult, part adolescent – who finds success "boring", who has a charming wife and delightful children yet wants to throw all this away. Sad that it seems impossible to give advice, even to one's best friend.'

Balfour sat still on the bed for some minutes in the semi-darkness pondering this verdict, then his eyes were taken again by the pile of books. From this angle he could see that a piece of paper projected from one of the books. It was a calf-bound first edition of Sir Thomas Browne's *Urne Buriall* that he had given to Sammy. When he opened it he found a small photograph and a piece of paper torn from a desk diary. He took them to the window as the light was so bad. The snapshot was of a group of men in battle-dress standing in front of an armoured car. At first he thought it was possible that Sammy might be one of the soldiers and peered closely at them all in turn. In June 1940 Sammy had seen a poster recruiting men for the Pioneers showing a foot treading on a swastika and the legend 'Step on it', and had joined up half an hour later when he was told that aliens were accepted. But as Balfour continued to study the photograph he saw that the soldiers wore Royal Armoured Corps berets, and one of the officers had a white webbing revolver holster of the kind issued to tank crews. He turned the photograph over and found a list of names including Captain L. K. Green, but it was another one which jumped out at him as if it had been printed in red capital letters: Sergeant

Patrick J. Quarry. Excitedly he scanned the diary. There were a few elliptic notes in Sammy's hand. 'Monday, 18th July. After lunch to a sale at Clapham Common with Jake Steiner. Property of the late Colonel F. K. Green, D.S.O. Quite a lot of looted stuff from Germany(?). Mysterious find in the cellar – Mannheimer drawings. Papers lead me to believe that these were acquired –? but where – by the Colonel's son who was a Captain in 1945. Duke's Own Hussars. Found a letter to him from a man called P. J. Quarry who served with him. Quarry a rare name and probably easy to find – then I want to trace Captain Knollys Green of the Duke's Own Hussars. Jake will check in Holland on the Mannheimer collection.'

17

Balfour woke from a tantalizing, vague dream to do with a locked door and glimpses of Ruth Connolly's nacreous skin, in which time had been mixed up so that he was excessively young to cope with the sexual aplomb of Mrs Alec Connolly. So be it. If sexual frustration was to be his lot from now on he could expect to have quite a few dreams of this kind.

In a supernal deific state of mind the distant noises of the traffic below hardly impinged while he half-heartedly tried to reconstruct the dream to make some sense of Ruth Connolly's appearance in a semi-maternal form, but he did hear a sharp rat-tat as the porter pushed his mail through the letter-box. Whatever fell on the mat made no noise at all. 6th August, 1966: it seemed as though his forty-third birthday had aroused scant attention. When he went to the door he found three cards, all with seaside views. He made some coffee and then read the cards with mixed feelings of pleasure and self-irony.

There was one from his aunt in Torquay who had brought him up: she had never loved him but had always been just and usually kind. Now, looking back, he was inclined to view their relationship differently. Why should she have felt deep affection for her brother's son, particularly as he had never been able to show much for her?

A prospect of the Citadel at Calvi and, on the other side, a scanty five-line message from Bunty confirming that, out of sight, he was practically out of mind. Somebody else must be continuing her lessons in water-skiing, skin-diving and other pleasurable subjects. There had been plenty of replacements hanging around. *Cosi sia*.

It was by a happy stroke of timing that the birthday card from Prudence had arrived on the day it celebrated. It showed a view from Axel Munthe's villa San Michele in Anacapri and Prudence inquired if he remembered the day when they had visited it together in 1963. Her card was nearly as brief as Bunty's but something about it told him that the verdict might not be in, that possibly he might be able to patch things up. He decided to go round to Orme Square and see Barbara in the next day or so – he had the excuse of taking the presents he had bought in Corsica for Prudence and Toby.

When he got to his office he found the mail delivery there had been skimpy too – two sale catalogues, a statement from his bank and a handful of letters. Patricia Bowyer and Jane Lupton did not work on Saturdays, but there was a note on his desk from Patricia: '4.30 p.m. Friday. Superintendent Hanson phoned to say that the Inquest will be held at Westminster Coroner's Court on Tuesday, August 9th, 10 a.m. He would like to see you there if possible, though it is very likely that after identification and the doctor has given cause of death the inquest will be adjourned.'

Balfour went through most of the letters quickly, but the printed heading of a bulky one on cream laid paper took his attention. There were two closely typed quarto pages headed 'Jacob Steiner Old Paintings & Master-engravings' with an address in P.C. Hooftstraat, Amsterdam.

4th August, 1966

Dear Mr Balfour,

I do not know if you have heard my name from Mr Samuel Weiss. I would not claim to be a close friend of his but he has been in the habit of visiting my shop over a period of years, occasionally taking coffee with us, and it was a great shock both for my wife Esther and myself to read the announcement of his death in *The Times*.

I have only recently returned here from a month's buying trip. When I was in London Mr Weiss escorted me on a visit to some galleries in the St James area and pointed out your office in Jermyn Street. My reason for writing to you is that I am deeply concerned in case his death should be linked in any way with a mysterious occurrence that took place during my visit to England. I shall now relate the circumstances and inquire from you what action you think I should take.

On Monday, 18th July I attended an auction sale with Mr Weiss at 'Eagle House', Cedars Road, Clapham Common, London SW4. I have the catalogue of this sale issued by Messrs Haley & Coote Ltd before me as I write and will be glad to send it to you if you wish me to do so. Mr Weiss had been told that the house contained some interesting things and this proved to be the case. It was apparent to us that most of the valuable items had come out of Germany and (from certain small points such as coats of arms, dates and signatures in books, etc.) we shared the view that this material might well have been looted in 1944/45. But, and this is the vital point, in the cellar at 'Eagle House' we came across some Mannheimer drawings – which very probably were *looted by the Nazis!*

Of course you may have heard of the famous collector Mannheimer but I must give you all the information I have even if it prove to be superfluous. Fritz Mannheimer was an exceedingly astute and wealthy Jewish banker (born in Stuttgart in 1891); he left Germany because of the Nazis and joined the old-established firm of Mendelssohn & Co. in Amsterdam. He used his financial genius to fight the Nazis and was consequently marked down for their special attention. But apart from being a financial wizard he was a collector of fine art and crammed his mansion in Hobbemastraat with beautiful pictures and, later, at Vaucresson, near Paris, the Chateau Monte Cristo.

On the 16th May, 1940 (the day after Holland surrendered), Reich Commissar Seyss-Inquart brought in his protégé, the art expert Dr Katejan Muehlmann with an organization called *'Dienstelle Muehlmann'*, to acquire pictures for the Nazis. Their principle was the axiom that all German works of art must return *'heim ins Reich'* but, as you will understand, this repatriation was interpreted very liberally. In fact various organizations such as 'Treuhand A.G.', 'The Adler Trading Company' and *'Einsatzstab Reichsleiter Rosenberg'* competed with notorious individuals like Hans Posse, Dr Erhard Goepel and Karl Haberstock (who made a fortune selling pictures to Hitler) for Dutch art treasures. In one month (December 1940) '*Dienstelle Muehlmann*' alone sent to Munich Pieter Breughel's 'Carrying the Cross', a Rembrandt self-portrait and two great Rubens portraits. Famous collections which suffered badly from Nazi depradations included those of Franz Lugt, Alfons Jaffe, Otto Lanz and the 'Gondstikker Collection' (some 1300 paintings) originally housed in the Kasteel Nijenrode.

I am not posing as an authority on this subject – I spent most of the war hidden in a friend's farm-house near Utrecht so I have little first-hand information of what happened in Amsterdam in 1940/1. And indeed the position there was so complicated by various factions – Ribbentrop had his own 'art battalions' while the '*Shantung Handelsgesellschaft*' pillaged for Göring – that it would require a specialist art historian to untangle it. But I do know that at the end of the war some of the stolen paintings were found in the Schloss Neuschwanstein, a hill-top castle built by Mad Ludwig of Bavaria. Many more, together with the bulk of Nazi lootings of bullion, magnificent jewels and tapestries, were discovered in the Alt Aussee salt-mine. This, the main repository, was fortunately reached by the U.S. Third Army before it could be destroyed on Martin Bormann's orders.

You can therefore appreciate our feelings on discovering these drawings in the cellar all stamped on their mounts to show the Mannheimer provenance. Mr Weiss was particularly intrigued – I think I should say obsessed – with the puzzle they posed. Then from some papers put aside for waste disposal in the cellar he decided that probably the drawings and the other looted (?) material had been collected by a certain Captain L. K. Green of the Duke's Own Hussars. We agreed to make inquiries: I would find out as much as possible about the actual disposal in Holland of the Amsterdam section of the Mannheimer collection, while Mr Weiss would track down the present whereabouts of Captain Green.

Now I am wondering (well aware that this may sound absurd to you) if it could be that his inquiries were connected in any way with his death. You may dismiss this suggestion as being wild surmise: certainly it is 'a shot in the dark' and perhaps you can straight away allay my fears, but I have been deeply puzzled and disturbed. I *do know* that when I last saw Mr Weiss, just three weeks ago, he was in fine spirits as usual and appeared to be in good health. I am sure you will understand my writing to you about my concern – when I was in London Mr Weiss spoke about you and I got the impression that your friendship was a close one. Please tell me your opinion. If there is any doubt in your mind do you think I should write to the police or will you contact them? In any case I shall look forward to hearing from you ...

It was a warm day but Balfour shivered suddenly and his hands were cold. Reading Steiner's letter, the conviction had grown in his mind that Sammy's death might not have been an accident or suicide – that Sammy, probing around in murky events of 1945, had uncovered a secret which had led to his murder.

Balfour pulled out the crumpled piece of paper which contained the rough chronology of events he had begun when he first returned from Corsica. Below the date when he had last seen Sammy he had added the day of the aborted auction at 'Eagle House' and the names Knollys Green, Quarry, Leonard K. G. Cato and Victor Maddox. Now he drew a dotted line linking all the names – he no longer doubted that there was a connection. He was not equipped to solve the mystery as Sammy had been – he did not have Sammy's chess-playing intellect or dozens of contacts in Jewish circles who might have useful information (he remembered that Sammy had once helped to track down a copy of the list of SS members – a book printed in an edition of fifteen copies, so rare that the Jewish Documentation Centre in Vienna had searched for one for years). What he did have was determination – the doggedness which had led to Max Weber paying him that left-handed compliment. He would try to find Patrick J. Quarry and see what he had to say about Leonard Knollys Green Cato, then he would pass on all his information to Superintendent Hanson.

18

The sun was shining from a cloudless sky and Balfour took off his jacket as he strolled slowly through Regent's Park. He took the circuitous outer path deliberately to kill time as he was anxious not to reach Camden Town before 2.15 p.m. He had spent most of the morning looking through the twenty-four volumes of *The Trial of German Major War Criminals* (Nuremberg), checking on references to looting, but had not been able to add to the information Steiner had given him. He had been more successful in tracking down Quarry's address: Patrick F. was the only private subscriber named Quarry in the London phone-directory with an address in the Star Mews off Gloucester Avenue, NW1. Balfour had lived in Camden Town for eighteen months just after the war and knew the short row of small Victorian cottages which made up one side of the Mews.

From Jermyn Street he had gone to a restaurant near Leicester Square but had found his plate of cold roast beef and salad completely tasteless – the suggestion of Sammy being a murder victim burned in him like a fever. Now, as he skirted Primrose Hill and dawdled along Fitzroy Road, he was barely aware of his route while his mind went on planning and re-planning a meeting with Mr Quarry. One of the main handicaps in following up Sammy's trail of inquiry was that he did not know what other things Sammy had found in the boxes of rubbish at Eagle House – and his brain was not functioning really clearly, being clouded with obsessive ideas of revenge. With all this in mind it was going to be hard enough for him to find a reasonable-sounding excuse for calling in at

Quarry's house, so he wanted to avoid reaching there at lunch-time.

Balfour put on his jacket as he turned out of Fitzroy Road into Gloucester Avenue, and nervously ran a smoothing hand over his hair. When he got to the corner of Star Mews he saw that the houses there were as small as he remembered them, probably built to provide the minimum living space required for ostlers or other workers employed at the Camden Town goods depot in the nineteenth century when the vast catacombs there swarmed with horse-drawn vehicles. Viewed up close, No. 7 Star Mews looked just like a doll's house. The miniature window frames were thickly covered with glossy yellow paint and the cement between the bricks looked as if it had been touched up with whitewash. A canary in a gilt cage was carefully positioned in the window to be in the sun and it trilled away unceasingly as he rang the bell. His hands were sticky and his chest tight as though he had embarked on some illegal project.

There was only a short pause before the yellow door swung open so that he could hear a loud Italian rendering of *A Hard Day's Night* and smell fried onion or garlic. A very tall athletic-looking man with a youthful face and lustrous grey hair filled the doorway, standing with his head lowered as if he was looking out from a manikin's stage set. Balfour asked 'Mr Quarry?' and the man gave a pleasant grin and nodded before he turned away and shouted: 'Concetta, turn it down a bit. A fractiony, *per piacere.*' The music ceased abruptly and he called out: '*Mille grazie.*' When he turned back he still had a friendly expression but there was a quizzical twist to it as if he half expected to be sold an encyclopedia.

Balfour cleared his throat and began an apologetic approach to the genial giant: 'Very sorry to bother you like this but I was hoping you could spare me a few minutes. My name's Balfour. Just a couple of questions. . . . Hope I'm not interrupting your lunch?'

Quarry dismissed all this with a shrug, said 'Finished',

and led the way into the tiny front room where the canary was singing away so loudly it seemed impossible that all that noise could come from an ounce or two of feathers. Quarry's casualness implied that the interview was not going to be of much importance or interest to him one way or the other. He collapsed into a chintz-covered arm-chair with a peculiar jack-knifing effect of his long legs and said: 'Have a seat. I know, I've won the pools and you want to break it to me gently.'

Balfour had been looking quickly round the room. The doll's house impression was exaggerated by the numerous small ornaments, but he liked the primitive coloured cast of the Madonna on the mantelpiece, the climbing plants and the very large white cyclamen on which the blooms looked like nuns' coifs. The furniture and the carpet were inexpensive. If Quarry had been in-volved with Cato in looting, his share of the booty must have been small. But everything about the man, his old tweed sports coat and schoolboy flannel trousers which showed a healthy indifference to appearances, his open face, his manner, led Balfour to believe that Quarry was free of deviousness and guilt. He abandoned his half-formulated sentences and decided to play the situation by ear. He took out the photograph of the soldiers grouped round the armoured car and handed it over with one of his business cards. 'No, not the pools I'm afraid. Simply wanted to ask you about this.'

Quarry shook his head, said, 'Well I'll be ...' then flicked on his infectious grin again: 'What is this? Some kind of treasure hunt? Can anyone join in? You see there was another bloke round here with a print of this same photo. Couple of weeks ago, so he has the lead on you. You're looking for the mysterious drawings too?'

'Oh, he told you about the drawings?'

'Yes. Nice little chap and he wrapped it up well at first. Very tactful he was but I definitely got the impression he thought my mob might have knocked them off. But I've nothing to hide. I'll tell you exactly what I told him. Fair enough? Mind you, I don't think you'll be much the wiser.'

'I'd be very interested even to know where and when the photograph was taken.'

'That's easy enough. Near Karlsruhe, April '45. Yes that's me, then Corporal, Acting Sergeant P. Quarry, Duke's Own Hussars, half asleep in the background. It's a bit of a joke really because I can see how you might think we were mixed up with all that Nazi loot. We were a reccy squadron. Reconnaissance, Military Intelligence. The nearest we got to the spot was Golling. Then we took a kind of Knight's move, one step forward and a jump to the side. Radstadt and up we shot into the Schladminger Mountains. We were rushing round and round there like mad. Up above Tamsweg. Trying to find "The National Redoubt". Remember all those rumours about the Wolf's Lair? How the Nazis were going to hole up in the mountains below Berchtesgarden and fight on? Lot of cock it turned out to be. "The National Redoubt" was a dream or a nightmare, depends on which way you looked at it. But anyway in the last week of April and first of May that was our job. And boy could we move then! We'd dropped the cars and were using U.S. 3rd Army's jeeps and half-tracks, liaising with them. We had no real fire power so if we hit anything big we shot off again like a fart in a colander. One day for instance we spotted the remnants of a SS Panzer Div HQ Column – just called in the 4th Armoured Shermans and they crucified it. But we never got to the saltmines at Alt Aussee, and that's the point, isn't it? Leastways that's where I heard the Nazis' treasure-trove was buried. What I do know for a fact is that Alt Aussee was taken by the U.S. 80th Infantry Div, and they sewed it up really tight.'

Quarry paused and held his head inclined to one side as though he was listening in case anyone was outside the door. 'I'll tell you one thing ...' He listened again. 'Best days of my life. Our mob was in on the Salerno landing and we had nine months in Italy before we came back to the U.K. for regrouping to go to France. I met the wife in Sorrento so I can't really complain about the Italian stint, but most of my active service was sweat, fright or sheer bloody boredom. Those last two weeks in Austria though, whizzing round the mountains, absolute chaos, the war ending, something happening all the time and yet no casualties – yes sir, those were the days.'

While Quarry had been happily reminiscing he had turned the photograph over. 'Hey!' he said sharply. 'This is the same photo the other chap showed me with all our names on the back. How come you've got it now?'

Balfour hesitated; he was wondering what explanation Sammy Weiss had given for having the snapshot. 'Well, it turned up in a lot at the auction sale with the suspect drawings and Mr Weiss bought it, then passed it on to me. I expect you know what dealers are like for selling among themselves, it's rather like taking in each other's washing ...'

Quarry interrupted him: 'You may think I've acted like a bit of a Noddy talking so much. But, as I said, I've nothing to hide. And frankly I didn't see why, still don't, anyone should think there's a connection between the photograph and the drawings ...' The sentence faded out on a note of doubt and his manner became slightly defensive: 'The little bloke, why didn't he tell you all this?'

Balfour lied easily: 'Well, I've bought the lot now, and if I want to give the drawings a provenance that's my problem. Looks as if I shan't be able to though.'

'I see. There's one more thing I said to the other chap so you might as well know it too. That cushy period I was talking about, there was a reason why it was so short for me quite apart from the war ending. On the 6th May, 1945, I was finished as far as the Duke's Own were concerned. *Kaput*. Went through a windscreen when I crashed a jeep in a river. At Bretstein in the Rottenman Mountains. Went back to Salzburg the next day in a lorry with a broken arm and ankle. My demob number came up while I was still in hospital at Guildford, so I never saw the old Duke's Own again.'

Quarry paused but Balfour said nothing. Quarry grinned knowingly and handed back the photograph: 'There's the difference between you and the other chap. Jewish, isn't he? When I told him that he was off again like a flash, looking for another trail. Did I know where he might contact anyone else who was in my mob? Where had they gone after Bretstein? Had to tell him that I haven't heard of or seen any of them in the last twenty-one years. But by the way he went off from here I felt he'd soon be ferreting out Captain Green's present address. Captain Leonard K. Green and yes, there was a Staff Sergeant Peter Bailey, Intelligence Corps, who was on our strength then. They were the brains of the outfit and they both spoke German like natives. If you could find either of them ...'

'Thanks very much. I'm grateful. But I won't take up any more of your time.' Balfour got up and in two steps was by the door to the passage. When he opened it he could hear a woman quietly singing a cheerful Italian song, and for a moment he looked round the little room again in which everything seemed to sparkle or shine, envying Quarry who had made his marriage a success instead of stalemate.

As he walked to the end of Star Mews he was disturbed by how little factual evidence he had to give Superintendent Hanson. There was the letter from Steiner, that was important, and Mr Stanley Coote would have to confirm that a number of suspicious items has been included in the Eagle House sale and then withdrawn at the request of a certain relative of Colonel Knollys Green, so Leonard Cato could definitely be linked up with that. But the other connections, though they now seemed very likely in his own mind, were really tenuous and hard to substantiate. And when Hanson set out to prove them, how many dissembling intermediaries would there be?

As he came to the end of Star Mews Balfour looked up

on hearing his name called out in an East London accent, contracted so that it was barely recognizable. 'Borlf! Here, Borlf. We want you.' It was a taunting tone and the command was uttered by the taller of Maddox's youths, the one who had leant so hard on Balfour's right arm; he now barred the exit to Gloucester Avenue but did so in a negligent manner, with his arms akimbo. He was dressed in a short jacketed Italian-style dark blue suit, and with his expressionless face he looked like a dummy in a Carnaby Street window.

'Come here, Borlf.' The youth addressed him again like a dog. Anger was a thing to avoid. He could see that the blue Ford Galaxie was parked about fifty feet away in Gloucester Avenue, and Victor Maddox was sitting in the driver's seat beckoning him contemptuously with a black-gloved hand. Losing his temper now would mean trying to fight three thugs and 'Don' the sadist, and would have a predictable conclusion. He needed to think clearly and run fast. Fortunately he was not off guard as he had been at Hyde Park Place – he knew both his opponents and the topography of Camden Town.

Balfour sniffed, then, grinning widely, walked up close to the youth. He knew the grin must appear highly artificial for he was mentally trying to duplicate Stanley Laurel's fatuous optimism, but it worked as the young man waited for him without taking his carefully posed hands from his hips. Apparently he accepted the fact that the dog 'Borlf' was coming back for more treatment. He began to move only when Balfour took one step more than was necessary for normal conversational purposes and hit him with jolting right and left jabs. They were short but damaging punches and the youth's hands came round to clasp his modish jacket as he staggered forward, landing on one knee.

Balfour looked past the fallen youth for a moment to the car where Maddox was half-way out on to the pavement, big beery face congested with anger, then whirled round and sped away, his heart pounding like some overworked machine. His breathing was rapid and absurdly loud like a bellows but he did not feel really nervous, just keyed-up and excited as he would be at tackling a dangerous ski-run or a difficult dive. Before they could slap him around again they had to catch him and where he was going the Ford Galaxie could not follow. He turned left and went through a short row of parked cars. He stopped for a second and heard somebody sprinting after him – it would be the other youth, not Victor Maddox or 'Don'. He heard his name again – this time shouted in a high, nervously belligerent voice, coupled with some indistinguishable threat.

Racing round a large lorry into the goods-yard, Balfour was surprised for a moment to see that there was no one in the usually busy fore-court, but then he remembered it was Saturday afternoon. On his right hand there were the shallow steps down to the tunnel leading to Chalk Farm Road and the labyrinthine net-work of underground passage-ways like a giant honeycomb. After a moment's hesitation he sped down the steps past the ancient notice proclaiming ALL HORSES MUST BE LED THROUGH THIS TUNNEL. Running into the gloom from bright sunlight he felt practically blinded – the tunnel was lit only by one very inadequate electric-bulb and a small amount of daylight seeping down through a few dust-laden circular grilles.

He found a place in the darkest part of the tunnel, then flattened himself against the wall. The sound of pounding footsteps became louder as his pursuer did not stop at the beginning of the tunnel but ran along it pell-mell. Balfour hit him with a very short punch, using the youth's momentum to provide the power. As the young man stumbled on helplessly Balfour punched him again, this time solidly with a right upper-cut which snapped his jaw shut with an unpleasant hollow noise.

Balfour stepped over the inert body, retraced his steps for a way along the tunnel, then climbed over a single plank barring the entrance to one of the small passage-ways leading off to his right. It was damp and smelled faintly of urine. The only sound was the continual drip of water. Blundering along in the dark Balfour crashed into a brick pier so that his right arm was seared with pain, then felt numb. After going only a short distance he turned off right, ducking under a half-lowered iron portcullis gateway into another, parallel, passage-way. He looked along it, and then walked back towards the main tunnel as he could just make out that its entrance was blocked with planks of wood so that he would be invisible to his pursuers even when they passed a few feet from him. The chances of their finding him were remote. It was too dark and there were too many passages for them to hope to make a successful search.

When he got to the end of the passage and stood with his left hand on the rough planks, Balfour had a brief sensation of claustrophobia, a moment's panic when the supply of air seemed insufficient. It was also foul to breathe and seemed to be impregnated with soot. He kept swallowing and licking his lips. The silence about him was somehow more intimidating than the noise of the chase had been.

Straining with his head right against the planks he could hear the youth groaning then retching, with faint sinister echoes. He had little feeling of compunction but it was still a relief to hear footsteps in the tunnel and then Victor Maddox's loud angry voice: 'Someone's here. Christ, it's Pete! He's right out. Sit him up. O.K. then Don, that Balfour's for a proper marking. Definitely. I don't intend to get my collar felt for that git. I'll really stop him this time.'

Whoever replied to Maddox spoke so quietly that Balfour could not pick up what was said. Then Maddox said in a very serious threatening voice: 'And *I* say he'll have to be stopped.' This seemed to arouse some argument from the quiet voice but Maddox cut in again quickly. 'Don't tell me your troubles, I've got my own. *I'll tell you* what's going to be done.'

There were some more subdued phrases which Balfour did not catch but he could hear Maddox's enraged retort and it hit him like an unexpected blow in the face. 'Oliver Gerrard? All right you see your "friend" Mr Gerrard. But just make quite sure he understands the position. I tell you straight that if this nosey —er Balfour isn't stopped right now we shall all end up doing some porridge.' On hearing Gerrard's name Balfour experienced a sick feeling of shock, as if he were going to be physically ill.

Holding on tight to the grimy planks he heard the other voice properly for the first time – it was shaky and raised on a note of nervous tension: 'Now for God's sake, Vic – think! Don't do anything drastic – just wait a bit. I must see Gerrard first and I don't know where to find him. Saturday afternoon, he won't be at work.'

'Find him?' Maddox snarled and Balfour could visualize colourless flat lips stretched over the big uneven teeth, and the narrowed plucked nostrils. 'I don't give a tuppenny — how you find him. Go round to all your special clubs. Hammer on the door of his fancy house in Seymour Street. You find him, Don, you're responsible. Look, your "friend" Gerrard, he got us into this, right? We did the job for him, right? He said put the Jew boy out of the window and scare him silly, right? So now I'm saying we've got to protect ourselves. Right?'

19

'Feeling all right?' Balfour looked up, slightly dazed, at the small Italian waitress, not sure whether she was being sympathetic or sarcastic because he had taken so long over his small cup of black coffee. Then he saw her gaze was directed at his right hand. The knuckles were badly grazed but dry – a little blood oozed from a gash in the fleshy part of his thumb, one of several small cuts self-inflicted during the tunnel chase that he couldn't really account for.

'Yes, thanks. I'm quite O.K.' He picked up the big menu in a reflex, defensive action but could hardly take in the violet copperplate words, let alone find anything he would enjoy eating, even though he knew the food was supposed to be good in this Italian-style café. The seat at the pavement table was ideal for watching Gerrard's house and all he wanted to do was sit on a little longer undisturbed. 'Can I have another coffee, please? *Cappuccino* this time.'

When the waitress had gone and he looked again down Wigmore Street to the French-grey painted door of Gerrard's house Balfour realized he was being regarded with curiosity by another, older woman standing just inside the café doorway. It was possible that they thought he had been knocked down in a street accident and needed assistance. Most of the three hours which had dragged by since he had emerged from the tunnel into Chalk Farm Road had been taken up with watching the Seymour Street door after ringing the bell there without any response, but he had spent a few minutes in the Oxford Circus tube station having a wash and ineffectually trying to brush his suit. The right sleeve was slit and he had been able to remove only a little of the tar-like grime. His shirt cuffs were stained with blood and dust. He met the older woman's eyes until she turned away. He did not care much for sitting around looking and feeling like a tramp but he had already killed over an hour walking up and down Seymour Street, re-reading the memorial plaque on Edward Lear's house until he knew it by heart, looking at his watch a dozen times, pretending to be intrigued by certain aspects of Portman Square.

He had found that he could not bend his arm properly and was wondering if the elbow was damaged – it throbbed continually. But it was not this pain which had induced the insidious sensations of nausea and weakness in his legs. He could remember his first boxing instructor at school telling him that there was nothing to be frightened of in being 'hurt a bit. After a moment you don't feel much. A little blood and snot. Nothing.' Balfour had proved this for himself in some fights during his army service and knew he could stand up to physical pain reasonably well. It was the knowledge that Oliver Gerrard had instigated Sammy Weiss's murder that had made him feel sick and weak.

A red Mini-Cooper was pulling up at Gerrard's house. Someone got out and stood by the grey door for a moment slightly bent down, waving as the car drove off. Balfour put two half-crowns on the table and walked off quickly, taking in some deep breaths. Striding along he was not conscious of his painful arm and his mind was strangely blank as if he did not know where he was going.

Standing by Gerrard's house Balfour hesitated a while, rubbing the back of his left hand across his mouth. What would he do if he was convinced that Gerrard had arranged for Sammy to be killed? He touched the circular stainless steel number plaque with his right hand and his fingers felt numb as though he would be able to smash them against the charcoal-coloured briquettes without feeling anything. When he pushed the bell there was a kind of mechanical groan close to his ear and then: 'Yep. Gerrard here. Who is it?' The voice came over an Entryphone – slightly distorted by the speaker, it sounded bored and mocking.

Balfour took a deep breath before speaking. He had to excise all feeling from his voice, as if he were trying to think himself into a stage character. 'Hello. It's Ned, er, Balfour. I – can you see me for a moment?' The contrived casualness sounded hopelessly false in his own ears but not apparently to Gerrard as he replied in a more cheerful voice which combined hints of mystification and amusement. 'Well! What a surprise! By all means – enter. The door openeth by magic. I'll be down in a sec.'

Balfour found himself in a long narrow hall at the end of which stood a life-size bronze reproduction of Donatello's David bathed in strong light. On a small table there was a silver bowl filled with freesias. From a room above he could hear a record of Sinatra singing *Strangers in the Night*.

When Gerrard appeared on the amber-coloured stairs he was cradling a Siamese cat in one arm. Instead of his usual dark grey suit he wore bleached jeans, white canvas shoes and a dark v-necked pullover without a shirt. With his free hand he straightened the edge of his pullover and said in a deprecatory tone: 'Imagine – I've been boating on the river! Boulter's Lock. Most unusual for me, but rather enjoyable. An Edwardian interlude.' His face was composed but his heavy lidded eyes were wary. When Balfour said nothing in reply, Gerrard smiled steadily and advanced along the hall with all the confidence of a skater expert on thin ice.

After keying himself up for this moment, Balfour suddenly felt terribly weary as though he would be unable to go through with it. He was aware of a dichotomy in his thinking – one force was urging him on to probe deeper into the mystery but another shunned and obscured the suspicion that was growing ever stronger. His silence in response to Gerrard's banter went unnoticed as there was a moment's diversion while the cat held in Gerrard's arms struggled violently, wrestled itself free and bolted back upstairs. Gerrard shot Balfour a puzzled look, said, 'That's odd. You don't loathe 'em, do you?' then shrugged.

Apart from the golden glow enveloping the Donatello bronze the hall lighting was subdued, coming from oblong panels of blue glass in the ceiling, and Balfour was standing in the shadow, turned away so that his torn sleeve was hidden. Gerrard pointed through a small passage-way off to his right: 'Let's have a drink. Myself, I could quaff about half a bucket of Campari Soda. How's that for you?'

There was another bronze in the passage, a reproduction of Cellini's Perseus holding a decapitated head on high in his left hand and a short sword in his right. As he passed the statue Gerrard's hand dropped caressingly on to the sword-arm and said, 'Ware this barbarity.' There was again a small commotion as another Siamese cat shot out of the dining-room. Gerrard nervously raised both hands in protest and grimaced unhappily.

The dining-table was a slab of hammered glass about six feet long supported on a frame-work of white wrought iron with matching chairs. A horse's skull carved from old ivory stood on the table as a centre-piece. A steel and glass trolley was loaded with bottles. A nervous-sounding little French gilt clock ticked away noisily on the Adam mantelpiece. There was an eighteenth-century Venetian Veduta painting; a sea-green Turkish rug on the oak parquet floor.

Balfour said quietly: 'I spent part of the morning with one of your friends.'

The innocuous-sounding sentence somehow ended up full of menace. Gerrard hesitated before replying, and a false provocative smile became affixed to his face. He pretended to busy himself with the paraphernalia of the drinks-trolley, but was obviously giving himself time to think. Then he straightened up: 'Oh, who was that?' He made his inquiry more casual by adding, 'And now, what to drink?'

Suddenly a picture of Sammy Weiss being forced out of the high window by Maddox and his hooligans blotted out the aesthete's room in Balfour's view. He lunged forward and pushed Gerrard, catching him off balance so that he crashed into the trolley and then fell to the ground, sliding along helplessly on the polished wood floor. When Gerrard turned his face was so transformed as to be hardly recognizable – the usual polite, slightly superior, mask had been replaced by a contortion of hatred and malice. He crouched warily, looking as if he might spring forward like one of his cats. But his words showed that he realized the futility of physical combat with Balfour. 'You bloody madman! What was that in aid of? Cretin. You absolute-stupid idiot! You'll get out! Now!' The ring of defiance in his voice was strained, but Balfour had the impression that Gerrard was experienced in the matter of awkward scenes, hysterical 'tiffs' which turned violent.

'I'll answer your other question first,' Balfour said in an unemotional voice. Now the messy business had actually started he was feeling calm and able to deal with it. 'Your friend that I met was "Don". And *his* friend Victor Maddox.' He moved his stiff right arm forward slightly. 'I got this escaping from them. But I overheard Maddox saying that you arranged that Sammy Weiss should be killed.' He held out his left fist threateningly. 'Now I'll tell you something else. Before I leave here I'm going to find out why.'

Gerrard propelled himself forward in a desperate dash for the door, but Balfour got hold of him by the neck and slung him back as easily as if he was disposing of a cushion. Balfour shook his head sadly: 'That was the wrong answer. And by God I hoped that you had the right one.'

Gerrard advanced slowly, holding the white-painted wrought-iron standard lamp like a shield in front of him, and then pushed it forward. Balfour sprang aside but the tip of one of the glass candles caught his cheek, scoring it lightly as though he had been cut by a blade of grass. He pointed to the ivory-handled knife on the trolley and said: 'You'll have to do more than that. Get the knife. You'll need it. Maddox said he was going to "stop" me. But now you've got to do it. You must stop me or talk.'

Balfour leaned forward and negligently hit Gerrard with a left jab in the chest. It was a pulled punch – the superimposed image of Weiss's killing had faded and he was not enjoying baiting Gerrard. The fight was too one-sided and was like the bullying he had undergone at Maddox's hands in Hyde Park Place. He licked his lips. He was loath to hit Gerrard again. Then he realized that Gerrard was collapsing, slowly sliding down the wall, rubbing his chest distractedly. Sitting on his haunches against the wall Gerrard gave a long-drawn-out groan and said: 'It was an accident. *Not murder!* Of course they didn't mean to kill him. We just wanted them to frighten him – that's all. To scare him – to stop him talking.'

'Who's we?' It was the question and answer that Balfour had subconsciously feared. 'You and Maddox?'

'It was Max.' The three words were like the crucial movement on a telescope lens that turns a blur into a clear focus. In a sharp moment of recognition the shadowy suspicions that had lurked in Balfour's mind all afternoon were confirmed and he saw a cinema of past events: Phyl Weber's dramatically changed appearance and her nervous greeting when he had returned from Calvi; Max's curious expression and the exaggeration of the story about the customer's adulterous wife; Max's eyes when he had said: 'Such things can happen quickly. They boil up – get out of control.'

'Max! But why? Why should he want to stop Sammy talking? About what?'

Gerrard waved a hand as if appealing for a truce. 'Just remember it was an accident. They put him out on the ledge all right – to *scare* him. But then he moved along out of their reach. They were trying to get him back when he fell. God! What are we going to do now?' He put his hands over his ears and rocked to and fro, swearing in a monotonous unbalanced voice.

Balfour pulled his hands away. 'What was Sammy going to talk about?'

Gerrard said despairingly, 'Oh God.' Then he looked up. 'He'd found out – oh – old stuff about Max's past. Apparently he came across some drawings at a sale that were linked up with Leonard Cato. Weiss knew they had originally been taken from a Jewish collection. So then he went on and on digging. He appointed himself a one-man investigating team – discovered that Max owned shares in Toller, Cato and learned Cato was a partner in Max Weber Ltd. And eventually he found out ... Max wasn't in a concentration camp. ... He – worked for the Nazis during the war, for Rosenberg, on his special staff collecting works of art. In April 1945 Max went to earth with a convoy of looted material. In a mountain village, near Freisach in Austria. Just after the war was over, at the end of May, Leonard Cato, who was in some special army unit, dug him out. When Cato heard about the barns full of loot he came to an arrangement with Max. Max was smuggled out of the country into Switzerland and they became partners. Max had been wounded in the face and he had some plastic surgery. Cato fixed him up with false papers to show he'd served a short sentence in Buchenwald as a Catholic protestor against the Nazis.'

'But how did Sammy find this out?'

'By probing and probing into Cato's background. He went to the Registrar of Companies and found out that Cato owned fifty per cent of the shares in Max's business. Then he came across a man called Peter Bailey who had a grudge against Cato and thought there had been some dodgy business in '45. And he turned up people who had been in Buchenwald. ... From the way he persisted you would have thought he was on the trail of someone in charge of an extermination camp instead of selecting pictures. Then he threatened to expose Max and Cato. They offered him money – said they'd make reparations of any reasonable kind. But he wouldn't listen. What good would it have done, really, for Max and Cato to be ruined?'

Balfour turned to leave the room but Gerrard called out: 'Don't forget. It was an accident, Weiss's death. Not murder.'

Balfour said contemptuously: 'Don't tell *me*. It's the police you'll have to convince.'

20

In the taxi from Seymour Street Balfour felt as though he was suffering from a fever. The excitement, the revelations and the continuing tension of the day had proved too much for him, resulting in a kind of nervous crisis – his hands trembled, his head ached and his face was hot.

Gazing out at familiar streets he could hardly recognize them – everything was unreal – it was as though he had lost all sense of orientation or was being driven through a nightmare world in which places were arbitrarily moved or changed. He looked on the Saturday evening strolling crowds with a jaundiced eye and the impression that he had been cut off finally from such normal pleasures. It was the confrontation that lay before him at Carlos Place that had finally brought on this mental malady: in his mind's eye there was always the tableau of Gerrard squatting on his haunches, his face contorted in a rictus of hatred, mouth agape to speak the fateful three words.

As the taxi pulled up at some traffic lights he noticed two young couples laughing in front of a florist's window and regarded their gaiety with a cold critical eye as if he was a visitor from another planet.

Even Carlos Place looked unfamiliar and when the taxi stopped the driver had to turn round saying 'O.K. Here we are then' before Balfour got out. As he did so, the muscles round his solar plexus contracted and he wondered if he would be sick. While the taxi disappeared he stood looking across at the Connaught Hotel, waiting until a little of the tension drained away.

Pressing the door-bell by the Padauk door he said aloud unbelievingly, 'Three days ago!' It seemed incredible that it was Wednesday that he had come to this door making an apologetic entrance, greeting Phyl with a kiss and asking his naïve questions of Max about Sammy. For a moment he felt giddy and the world seemed topsy-turvy – nothing made sense and anything might happen.

The heavy door opened slowly and he saw Phyl Weber. This time she did not offer her cheek to be kissed but shrank away with a startled expression as if he might hit her. He could see that she had been crying and knew that Gerrard must have phoned. She looked old and ill. With one hand she clenched a scrap of lace and with the other made a small tentative gesture of despair. Without a word he walked past her and the stone inscription which now had such an ironical ring: LET EACH MAN TAKE UP HIS CHISEL AND INSCRIBE HIS OWN FATE.

He had thought of many bitter things to say to Phyl but they had vanished on seeing her. She was super-sensitive, her emotions always near to the surface, and these events must have already had a terrible effect on her – and she had been only an unwilling spectator, unable to affect the outcome.

'Where's Max?' he said, without turning to look at her.

'Oh Ned! I wanted to talk to you. Max isn't here. You must let me explain. You must understand – you know that Max wouldn't ... He was sickened by what happened.'

Balfour turned, shaking his head sadly. 'I know exactly what happened, and I do understand, I'm afraid. Max's reputation, his possessions, his fabulous career were at stake. Obviously nothing could be allowed ...'

Phyl intervened: 'But Sammy was trying to make him a scapegoat for all he had suffered in the past. Max was just an art expert, not a member of the Death's Head SS.'

Balfour ignored her repetition of Gerrard's argument, continuing as if she had not spoken: 'Max's career would have been finished, he might even have had to go back and stand trial for the offences he had committed. And his attempt to bribe Sammy failed. So naturally, those thugs were turned loose to terrorize. ... Do you know the supreme irony of the whole thing? Sammy hadn't even made up his mind about denouncing Max. Yes, it's true! He sent me a cable in Corsica saying that he wanted my advice on his "terrible decision". You see? But of course Max could not take a chance. And now Sammy's dead.' Balfour walked on towards the stairs saying in a loud voice: 'Where's Max? Is he hiding up there?'

'Wait, Ned. Talk to me – *please*. I told you Max isn't here.'

Balfour nodded like a mechanical doll. 'I know. But you lied to me the last time I was here.'

He ran up the stairs and went along the landing, opening all the doors and finding the rooms dark and empty.

There was another flight of stairs leading to the Weber's private apartment, and he had begun to climb these when he heard noises in the hall below. Voices raised in argument, in particular Phyl's, sounding shrill and hysterical. Then another, louder noise as if the ebony and bronze door had been flung back jarringly against the wall. Physical violence of any kind was not like Max, and Balfour was puzzled. He went back to the top of the first flight of stairs.

Victor Maddox, one of his young toughs and another man, tall and lean, were standing there arguing with Phyl – Maddox underlining some point by jabbing his finger at her. Balfour shouted: 'Don't do that!'

Maddox looked up and called out: 'Why, it's friend Balfour! Now you come down here. We've just been round to Seymour Street and found you had beaten us to it. So come along down, friend Balfour. I've got someone else for you to play with.'

He indicated the third man, lantern-jawed, in a navy serge suit a size too small for him, who was standing about aimlessly with his hands in his pockets. Maddox put both hands in a proprietory manner on the tall man's shoulders and shouted to Balfour, 'Yes, just nip down and punch *this* lad in the stomach.' He urged the man up the wide stairs and the two of them advanced step by step together.

Balfour hesitated for a moment. His brain dictated that he should run into Max's office, lock the door, phone the police – logical action was quite plain. But anger was welling up in him – when Maddox had shaken his finger at Phyl, Balfour again visualized him forcing Sammy through the window. He shook his head as though to clear it and took a step down. Phyl Weber called out his name in a shaky, frightened voice but he was deaf to warnings now and blind to his surroundings. The only rational thinking he was capable of informed his fighting instinct. The tall blue-suited man held his hands low and his stance was the contemptuous one adopted by veteran boxers in fair-ground booths. Balfour felt sure that he would soon go down before those long wiry arms and practised fists. 'Thrice armed is he who gets his blow in fust.' He threw himself down the stairs, cannoning off the banisters and swinging a left haymaker at Maddox's big, congested face, using all his strength as if he was trying to fell a tree.

The punch seemed to explode in Maddox's neck but the next moment Balfour went down under a torrent of blows – so many that he did not know where they were landing or who was hitting him. He continued to descend the stairs, but in ridiculous slow motion, and it was a dream-like effortless activity. He lost consciousness without being aware of pain, as though he had been given a shot of Pentothal. There was an ever more distant voice calling his name over and over again, followed by a roaring noise in his ears that increased in volume until it became nearly unbearable, then nothing.

*

Balfour woke reluctantly to the moaning of tugs and the fainter sound of water slapping and washing against timbers. First the noises and then pallid light broke through his protective barrier. He returned to life with a deep feeling of distaste, it was like wakening from a nightmare to find that all its worst events turned out to be true. He lay quite still for a while going over the sordid hours which had led up to the drugging sleep.

When he twisted his neck slightly to see where the light came from he found it was stiff and sore. His ribs ached and responded to any movement like a devilish waistcoat devised by a torturer. Very slowly he got up into a sitting position. He had been lying on the floor close to the door of a narrow office. On his left there was a row of steel filing cabinets, to the right a typist's desk and chair and a window lit by the moon.

It was a disturbing feeling coming back to consciousness in utterly strange surroundings. He remembered a scene from wartime Italy: they had been going in convoy to cross the River Volturno above Caserta on the first of his few days of really active service. Forced to stop at an exposed point where the shelling was heavy, he had looked out and seen a G.I., an infantry sergeant, who grinned at him. Then the sergeant had nodded, waved a hand in the direction of the gunfire and called out 'Kinda scarey, eh kid?' This simple acknowledgement of their common feeling had stayed with him since and the trivial incident had borne him up in a few subsequent moments of fear. Now he said aloud, 'Kind of scarey, eh kid?' but it sounded like someone else mimicking his voice and the words echoed and buzzed in his ears.

A glance from the window showed him that he was in a building overhanging the Thames. He could easily pinpoint its position as he practically faced Billingsgate with Tower Bridge on his right hand and London Bridge to the left: one of the wharves off Tooley Street. Then a vignette flashed into his mind – the day when he had been standing on London Bridge and noticed the impressive Toller, Cato building near Hay's Wharf. He was a prisoner in it now.

He looked along to the right at a ship partly hidden by

a series of cranes, then gazed down to estimate how high he was above the river. Light was streaming from a window on the floor below him nearer to the side of the building. He was four floors up, perhaps fifty feet. Patiently searching the area below he saw a measure, like a giant perpendicular ruler, affixed to the end of one of the wharves, giving the depth of water up to twenty-one feet. It showed only the numbers above seventeen. Fifty feet into, say, sixteen feet of water. He had jumped from a greater height at Praiano for a hundred lire bet. Here the stakes were all-important and he had nothing to lose by not attempting it. He went to the door, tried the lock and listened intently. There was a good deal of distant argument, voices rising and falling.

When he went back to the window he carefully scanned the surface of the dark water. At Praiano he had been able to see exactly what lay below him. Here there might be a wooden platform or steps covered by the high tide. There was no guarantee that he would not hurtle down on to a hidden concrete slope. In a minute he might easily kill himself and so provide a ready solution for those who had brought him to Tooley Street. He took off his jacket, shoes and socks then padded back to the door once more and heard Max shout in an enraged voice: 'Now just go back again and bring Mr Cato with you. Nothing's to be done till he is here.' There was the noise of a door slamming and two or three people running downstairs.

When he was balanced on the window ledge, crouching awkwardly, Balfour had a giddy feeling as if he was already falling – the helpless sensation of vertigo which he had never experienced properly before. The water's surface, black with oily glints, seemed to shift suddenly then race up to meet him.

He hung back from the edge, unable to summon up the will to jump. It was his injured right arm that worried him – it would affect his balance and confidence. But there was something else – the height and the dark indefinite surface had a strange hypnotic effect as if they were willing him on to another purpose. Hanson had said that vertigo had been explained as the tension between the desire to fall and the dread of falling. Had Sammy, on the towering ledge, been tempted by death, the last best friend? The endless embrace, offering oblivion and release from the remorse that Sammy felt for his parents and sisters left behind to be butchered at Auschwitz.

Balfour sprang forward unsteadily and felt himself falling slightly backwards in the descent so that he entered the water as if he had come off a chute, struggling and sinking down in an ungainly fashion until his left foot hit the slippery mud bottom of the river. When he broke the surface he was choking and spitting but the water was not unduly foul. He lay on his back, kicking his legs up and down and paddling with one hand, making slow progress like an elderly gentleman bather till he reached some slimy steps.

Walking gingerly along the pitted concrete surface of the wharf on bare feet, Balfour felt better than he had done for several hours. The tension had gone, leaving him quite calm. He took some deep breaths of the fresh night air and stared up into the starlit sky, wryly remembering the last time he had looked at it – with Bunty. How absurd a picture he would make through some celestial telescope, shivering in his clinging wet shirt and trousers, a puny stupid figure trying to redress a squalid crime with yet more violence.

When he had opened the side door to the Toller, Cato warehouse he stood quite still in the shadowy hallway listening carefully in case Maddox had left the youth or his reserve bruiser behind, but the building was dark and quiet.

He found Max Weber on the third floor, seated at a large desk with two telephones. Max had a fixed expression of profound despair, like a psychotic, and seemed to be rooted there, lacking the will to move. He showed no surprise at Balfour's sudden and slightly comic appearance, simply letting his arms fall as Balfour locked the door behind him and saying: 'And so – it comes to this.'

Balfour stared at him for a few moments with a feeling of bitterness which was directed partly at himself. 'You know, Max, for a little while I had a cruel idea. I wanted to force you out of a window – to give *you* a taste of the terror that Sammy must have gone through. You may not have wanted him to die but you were quite willing to employ those thugs. You're a selfish bastard, indifferent to everyone else. I just hope I can learn a lesson from you. And now – I'm going to make Sammy's phone-call for him.'